Grace

Mail Order Brides of Wichita Falls

CYNDI RAYE

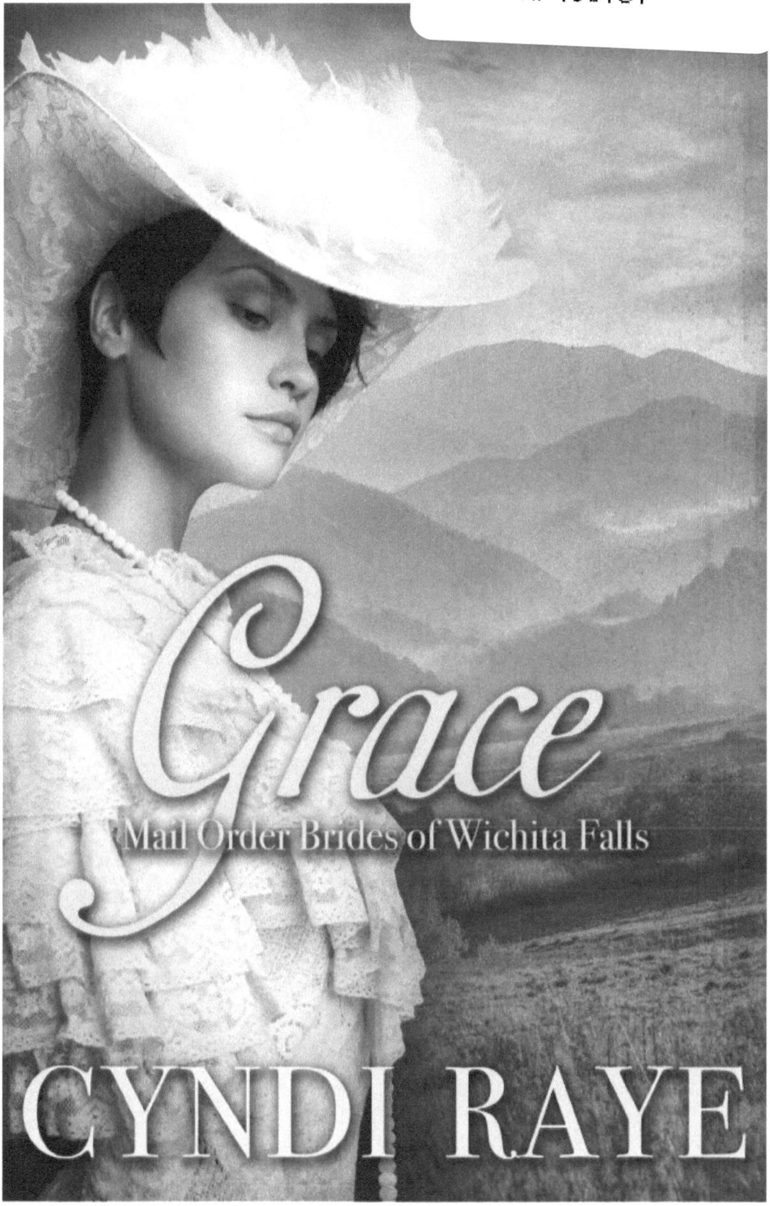

Grace
Mail Order Brides of Wichita Falls
Book 2
by
Cyndi Raye

*****

If you would like to become part of the reader's exclusive group, I have a free book for you. It's the story of Miss Addie and how she became the owner of the matchmaking company. Go to www.cyndiraye.com
Get your FREE story here! [2](http://www.cyndiraye.com/miss-addies-story/)

---

1. http://www.CyndiRaye.com

2. http://www.cyndiraye.com/miss-addies-story/

Chapter 1

Dawson pulled the rickety high-back wooden chair away from the desk, slinging a leg over the seat and sat down. He flung his arms over the back, pressing his forehead against the wood. It had been another long, hellish night. So bad, in fact, the dreams were so livid, he had tossed and turned so much it felt as if he was still in the horrible nightmare.

All he could hope is one day they would be gone. What he would do for a decent nights sleep. A heavy sighed left him. If they never ceased, then he would certainly suffer the rest of his life for what had happened. Either way, he figured he deserved to be tormented by the screams of the innocent family he practically had a hand in slaughtering. He knew in his heart he was innocent of the crime but if it hadn't been for him, they may still be alive.

With blurred vision, a shaky hand felt around for the top right desk drawer. He needed more, just a slug of whiskey to get him through the morning. He pulled back when the jingle of the bell above the door went off. Who would be at the land office so early? Dawson glanced at the clock, his heavy-lidded eyes trying to make out the numbers as he silently begged his foggy brain to wake up.

Who would be here at a quarter till eight in the morning? Whoever had the galls to grace his doorstep this early was lucky to find him here. On any other given day he'd still be at the saloon, sleeping off a long night of self-torture. Little did anyone know he wasn't there to buy women, but to drink his nightmares away. Lily was the only other person on earth who knew of his sickness. She'd been a good friend, even though her job as a serving girl wasn't the most acceptable or proper. But he liked Lily, like a sister. In fact,

Lily spoke more and more of leaving her job after she made enough money to start over away from the saloon.

He tried to help her many times, offered her money to leave but she refused each time, saying she'd do it on her own. The old owner gave her a small broom-closet like room off the kitchen with a bed and dresser. Every night, the two of them would sit in her room, far removed from the night-life of the saloon and gulp down whiskey until Dawson was so drunk he'd pass out in order to get through the nightmares. She would talk him through his troubles.

They were friends, doing each other a favor. A new owner had taken over recently and wanted Lily to turn tricks to pay for the room that was given to her by the prior owner since her wages didn't cover a room. So Dawson bought her every night, paying for her room and board so she wasn't forced to do what most women had to. Someday she would leave there,she swore. Most people gossiped about the two of them but he didn't care. Dawson had to do whatever it took to get through each horrible night.

He risked peeking at the front door. Five figures stood there, stoic, unsmiling. Dawson groaned. "What?" he croaked, his voice hoarse.

"We came here to help you, Dawson." His good friend Marshall Montgomery stood in the front of the pack, his legs slightly apart, hands in his pockets, a serious look on his chiselled face. The brim of his cowboy hat covered part of his brow. Beside him stood a miniature cowboy, Billy, his eleven year old nephew, who was wearing the same type of cowboy boots and hat, even down to a look-a-like button down shirt. The kid's hands were on his hips, staring along with the others.

Dawson flung his head back, running a shaky hand through his golden brown hair. "Help me? I'm not in need of help."

Reverend Daniel Conners and his serious wife stood side by side, their eyes on him, disapproval written all over their faces. "Tsk, tsk, now, Mr. Sloan, we've come to help your wandering ways. Besides, your brother is on his way here. Should be arriving shortly."

A moan slipped from Dawson's lips. "How shortly?"

"A month. You know what you promised him. Right now, you don't look like no married man, making this business respectable and becoming a rising citizen of Wichita Falls."

"More like a man who fell from grace, depending on a bottle of whiskey to get him through his day," Marshall told him straight out.

Dawson threw a fist in the air. "Get out, all of you. I don't need any help. I'll figure something out. Go on now, every single one of you, please, go." He laid his head back down against his arms, closing his eyes in hopes when he opened them again, the others would be gone.

No such luck. Raising his head, when he opened his eyes there they were, a motley crew, brows raised and frowning. "We're not going anywhere, Dawson. As your friends, we can't let you ruin your life."

"It's my life to ruin, not yours," he told Marshall.

"I've known your family a long time. Your brother trusted you to take care of his initial investment. He promised you the business if you could settle down and make a go of it. Now, I'm not so sure you ever heard him."

"I heard him alright." He wasn't about to tell any of them standing here how he could barely get through the day, let alone the night, guilt of what happened overwhelming his whole life.

The lady in the rear of the crowd came forward. He had a high respect for Miss Addie, proprietor of the local boarding house and long-standing citizen of their town. She brushed by the others and stood alongside of him. A soothing hand was placed on his shoulder. He turned his head. "Miss Addie," he said, starting to nod but then the pain shot up his neck to pound his skull again. He let his head flop back down.

"Dawson Sloan, I promised your brother I would look after you."

"No need for that, ma'am. I'm fine on my own."

"You certainly are not, young man. I find you abhorrently in need of a bath and a shave. It's time to clean up your act and make do on the promises you made to your brother."

"I was probably under the influence of some spirits when I agreed to his demands."

Her hand left his shoulder. "A promise is a promise. Imbibing in spirits will not make a difference to a man like your brother. He will hold you to your word. Gentlemen?" At her last word, two men came through the front door, the bell jangling, making his head hurt even more. They carried a wooden tub and set it dead center in the room.

Dawson watched them go back out only to bring in steaming pails of water to fill the tub. "What are you doing?" he asked Miss Addie. Although, he already knew. She was going to clean him up.

That'll be the day, he grumbled.

"I'll give you two choices. Either get in that tub yourself or these men here, they'll put you in there, clothes and all."

She wasn't joking. Not one lick. Dawson knew when a woman like her meant business. He looked to the others for help. "Marshall?" he begged.

Marshall shook his head back and forth. "No can do."

"Traitor," he mumbled, pushing back the chair as he stood, tottering on unsteady feet.

"Just doing what I should a long time ago," Marshall told him.

The bell jingled again. Marshall's wife entered, smiling as if she hadn't known what was going on here. She could barely hold her goods in her arms. Marshall immediately went to her, taking the packages. "Dang it, Ruby, I told you I would help you. In your condition, you should not carry too much."

Ruby took Marshall's face in her hands and pulled him in for a quick kiss. "It's not a condition, Mr. Montgomery. It's a baby."

"Everyone, out!" Dawson ordered. If he had to get in the tub, he darned well wasn't going to have an audience. For Pete's sake, they all acted as if they were here on a friendly visit. He gazed at the tub, thinking some hot water may actually clear his head.

Ruby smiled at Dawson, then the tub. Her hand went to her mouth, but he heard her whisper to her husband. "It's about time, I can barely stand the smell in here."

"Out!" he roared, grabbing both sides of his head and teetering forward.

Addie shooed everyone out, including the men who filled the tub with water. She turned back one last time. "There will be someone else stopping by after you bathe. The barber will get rid of the hair on your face. When you are finished, stop by. We have serious business to discuss."

Addie picked up her skirts and followed the others out. She took the knob in her hand and slammed the door, making Dawson's head ache even more. He began to strip off his shirt, swearing that she banged the door on purpose.

He strolled to the window, pulling down the blind to keep everyone from staring from outside as he undressed and stepped in the tub. Sinking in the hot water, he realized it did feel good. Heck, it felt great. So great in fact, he dozed in the water, not waking back up until he heard a pounding on the door. "It's open."

An older Chinese woman entered, holding a new set of clothes. She spoke in her native tongue, issuing orders to the young man who followed her. He took out a strait razor and held it close to Dawson's chin. Dawson jerked back at first, then relaxed as the boy began to lather up some soap and brush it across his whiskers. He stared at the boy, daring him to leave a cut on his skin. The boy didn't flinch at Dawson's stare. He seemed to be confident and before Dawson knew what was happening, the boy gave him a close shave that even he couldn't complain about. Next was a haircut, not too short but enough to make Dawson look presentable.

By the time the boy was finished, the bath water had cooled. He got out and dried off while the woman unfolded the clothes. He thanked her and motioned for them to leave. When they stood there, undaunted, he realized he had to pay them, too. "For Pete's sake. She orders me to clean up and expects me to tip, too." Dawson grumbled the whole time he took money out of his drawer, handing it over to the woman.

After they left, he took a look at himself in the mirror by the door. Staring into his dark bloodshot eyes, he remembered a day when he looked like this. Clean cut, not a whisker on his face, his honey colored hair neat and clean. His muscles ached from too much booze. Maybe it *was* time he tried harder.

Then he looked in to the mirror again and instead of seeing a handsome man trying to come back to life, all he recognized was a haunted man, guilty of a crime so heinous he couldn't sleep at night. Even though everyone said it wasn't his fault, Dawson felt in his heart it was.

He tore his eyes from the mirror towards the desk drawer. One drink. He turned towards the desk. In order to get through the rest of the day, he just wanted something familiar to help. Pulling the drawer open, he stared at the bottle lying on top of other papers stuffed in there.

"Let's go, Dawson. Quit yer dallying."

Dawson turned to see Marshall standing in the doorway.

He closed his eyes. Taking a deep breath, he pushed the drawer shut with a bang. Turning, he strolled towards Marshall, a look of disgust on his face. They were all out to help him, they'd said.

"It's a start," his friend said, knowing he made a hard decision to walk away from that drink. Marshall patted his back, a friendly move that had Dawson frowning.

"It won't do any good. Try all you might, but it won't do any good."

"We'll see. Let's go talk to Addie. She's got some good news."

Dawson went out in to the bright sunlight.

His friend stood beside him as he gazed in to the street. The town was busy, women and men walking down the street, horse's hooves clattering along, stirring the dust in the air. The sounds of everyday life was all around him.

Marshall told him, "Someone once told me it's a great day to be alive when the sun shines like so, Dawson."

Dawson stomped across the street to the boarding house. "Whoever it was, must've been drunk as a skunk."

<> <>

Tillo came through the back door and sat at the kitchen table. She looked at her daughter and smiled.

"What is it, Mother? Why do you look so sad?" Grace didn't like to see her mother looking so down and out. She gathered her mother's calloused hands in her own, sitting across from her at their small round table in the tiny apartment. It was all they had been able to afford.

"I have such sad news, honey."

"Oh, mother, is Mrs. Adams gone?"

Tillo let the tears fall down her cheeks. "She is. I took care of her for all these years. I don't know what I'll do without her now. She was my friend. At least one good thing came out of all of this and that is her daughter has a wonderful new life, with a baby on its way."

Grace smiled. She recollected how her mother took care of Mrs. Adams, her daughter Ruby and the Brownstone manor. Mrs. Adam's brother owned the manor and was always so mean. Many times Grace remembered how awful he was to Ruby. She had wanted to give him a piece of her mind, but her mother reminded her how much of a lady she was. Pooey!

Her mother never knew some of the naughty things her and Ruby would do. One time they added a bit of hot pepper to her uncles flask of bourbon. They laughed so hard when they heard him coughing and carrying on in his study after he took a drink. When he came out of the study to find out why his bourbon was so strong, they had been sitting on the steps of the front porch, two young girls acting all innocent. He had glared at them both before turning back into the house and slamming the front door.

She had some good times with Ruby as she was growing up. Grace was happy for her friend, sorry she was so far away but glad she found true love as a mail order bride. She hung on to her mother's hands a little tighter. They would get through this sadness. "Does Ruby know her mother is gone?"

Tillo shook her head. "Not yet. It will take some time to get word to her. Mrs. Adams lived longer than any of us expected. It's been over a year since Ruby has been gone. After she left, Mrs. Adams seemed to gather a second wind, getting up and moving around, sitting in the garden every day. I swear she was staying alive to make sure Ruby's life went on as planned. Every letter she received from her sister Adeline, she read over and over again, giving her a new lease on life. But it wasn't enough. She took a turn yesterday and left this life within hours."

"I'm so sorry, Mother."

"I know, thank you. I do have some other bad news. I'm no longer employed."

Grace was shocked. "Why?"

She shrugged. "Mr. Adams fired me on the spot. Said the only reason he kept me around was to keep his sister happy. The man is sick. I doubt by this time next year he'll even have a home. I am certain he'll lose it all, wind up in the poor house."

Grace nodded. Served him right, he was a mean and nasty man. "Don't you worry, Mother. I have a job at Montgomery Wards. I can help you now that I'm done with my schooling." Grace had gone to business school to learn accounting.The men made fun of her because they couldn't imagine a woman learning numbers. They said no one would hire a woman accountant. Perhaps they were right but she'd show them. She could work numbers like nobody's business. Hopefully a good job would come to her soon. Even though standing at a counter ringing up purchases at Montgomery Ward wasn't the type of job she longed for, it was a big help, especially now.

"Grace, you are always so positive, reaching for the best life offers. I'm afraid this time we are in a bit of a bind."

"Why, Mother? I said I can help."

Grace watched as her mother struggled for the right words. "I'm afraid without the salary from the Adams, I'm going to have to give up this apartment. I hate to break this news to you my darling, but my brother asked me to move to Georgia. He is in need of help with the children."

A stark fear ran through Grace. Then she shook it off. Why hadn't her mother said both of them? "What about me?" she whispered.

Tillo's bottom lip trembled. "There isn't room, Grace. I'm so sorry. Look, I won't go. We can get by here. You and me." A haunting look came over her mother's face.

Grace knew in that instant her mother wanted to go to Georgia. She wouldn't be the one to keep her from those dreams. After all, her mother had taken care of her for twenty-two years. She deserved a better life.

"No, Mother. You must go."

"I don't want to leave you here alone. Although, Miss Adam's sister from Wichita Falls has a booming business and offered you a position, of sorts."

"Of sorts?" Grace stared at her mother. Something sounded a bit off. "What kind of position?"

"Just like Ruby, you would be traveling to Wichita Falls," her mother said, softening her voice so Grace wouldn't get upset.

"As a mail order bride? Mother, that's the last thing I would want!" She stood and paced back and forth across the floor.

"This is a unique position, Grace. You would not only be a mail order bride but you would have a job with numbers." Tillo looked at her daughter with hope.

Grace stopped pacing. "What do you mean with numbers?" Her mother knew how she loved working with numbers, putting them together to make things work. Learning accounting had been fun and easy for Grace. But finding a job in New York City had been almost impossible. She had to face the truth, looking for a job while working at a department store was getting her nowhere fast. So many doors had been slammed in her face. Because she was a woman. Maybe she should listen to this offer.

Tillo smiled and reached for her hand. "Sit, Grace."

Grace did as told. "I love working with numbers, Mother. Perhaps I could consider this job. What does it involve?"

Tillo slipped her hand in to her pocket and extracted a train ticket. "This is not only a job but a new life, Grace. Wichita Falls is a growing town, where there are more men than women. It is growing by leaps and bounds with Miss Adelines careful picking of mail order brides. I know you will love the wide open plains and small town living. It beats these concrete walls and dirty city streets here."

Grace had yearned for a change. Now it was being presented right in front of her by her own mother. How could she refuse? Especially when she saw how her mother's eyes lit up talking about moving to Georgia. It was a new start, for them both. She sighed. "I'll do it."

Tillo grinned. "Even before knowing the whole story?"

"Well, by all means, tell me then."

"Your intended is a partner in a land title company, which he has sadly run in to the ground. His brother is the other partner and on his way to Wichita Falls to see if the business has improved. If it has, he intends to give his shares to his brother. The company is buying and selling land plots, Grace. That's right up your alley.

Surveying, working with numbers, it's a dream job come true for you. You know numbers, you would be a big help at a time like this. Imagine keeping the books for a business that you are a big part of."

"You know me well, Mother. I love to make a difference." The job sounded more than wonderful. The only problem was she'd have to become a mail order bride and move thousands of miles away. She looked around the small apartment. It was time for a change. For the both of them.

Chapter 2

If Dawson were honest with himself, he'd admit he felt a lot better than he had in months. Ever since the tragedy that spurred him to drown his sorrows in whiskey. Not that he wasn't a strong man, he was. There was something about feeling responsible for another life that could dig deep in your soul.

Dawson had let it get the best of him. No more. He wanted his brother to be proud of him. Sitting across from Miss Adeline, sipping out of a tiny English teacup was humiliating to most men. Except he wasn't about to refuse this woman who helped almost every single person in town. She was like an angel, bringing good tidings and joy to those around her. He'd sit here and dally any day. Besides, it beat drowning himself in his own pity now that his head was clear again.

"How is the tea?" she asked, nodding to the tea cup.

"Fine, Miss Adeline."

"The reason I asked you here is because I've taken a step without your permission and I must say I'm sorry but yet I'm not. I'll add that before we start."

"I don't understand."

"Of course not. Let me explain. You promised your brother by this time of year you would be settled down with a bride and your company would be booming. Can you face your brother knowing it isn't true?"

Shame crossed his face. "I got sidetracked but Ben will understand. He knows what happened."

Adelines all-knowing eyes bore in to his. "Not so fast, young man. He won't understand that you spend every single night at the saloon and drink yourself numb. Is that what you are doing, Mr.

Sloan? Trying to make the bitterness and shame disappear? How is that working for you?"

He sighed. "It isn't. If it weren't for Lily I'm not sure where I'd be right now."

"Lily? Little Lily Morgan?"

He nodded. "Everyone thinks I'm dallying with prostitutes but I'm not. Lily has a room off the kitchen the old owner gave her along with her serving job. But the new owner, she wants Lily to pay rent, trying to convince her to become a soiled dove for payment. Lily wants to move out but the job doesn't pay enough for her to leave. So, we devised a plan. I pay her to pretend I'm staying with her and she helps me get through the nightmares. She pays rent with the money I give her and is trying to save enough to leave there." Why he felt the need to spill his guts to this woman, Dawson didn't understand. Miss Addie had a way about her for sure.

"Everyone thinks Lily is a lady of the night. Why is she letting her reputation go sour, Mr. Sloan?"

"I don't know. She has her secrets but she won't tell. I've offered her money to leave there, to get on a train and go somewhere to start over but she refuses. Says this is her home. She'll dig herself out if it kills her, she told me. I'm not sure why she thinks she has to suffer so. Even so, she's my friend and she's helped me get through some pretty bad nights."

"Are you having nightmares?"

Dawson nodded. It pained him to talk about it so he clenched his hands around the tiny china cup.

"You're going to crush my teacup."

He looked down at his hands and released the cup. "I'm sorry."

Miss Adeline sighed. She reached out to take his hand. "Listen to me, Dawson Sloan. You have a brother who took care of you when your own parents died. He helped you through school and the two of you bought this land title business. He wants you to be a success but he's coming this way and if he sees the mess you are in, he's going to shut it all down and you will be left desolate. This is your last chance to make something of yourself."

"My brother can be a real jerk."

"Your brother loves you, Dawson."

"I've never been able to do anything great in his eyes."

"That's not true and you know it. He's had to grow up fast, wants the best for you. If he's hard to please it's because he is so busy trying to make sure you are OK. He's gotten you out of many troubling instances in your younger years and now here you are again."

"I would be fine if I hadn't hired that boy who was so green around the collar that day."

"You didn't know, Dawson. Life is too short to try to go back and replay things over and over. What happened is over and done with. Now it's time to go on living. I have just the thing. I ordered you a mail order bride."

He let go of her hand and sat back in his chair. "A what?"

Adeline smiled so sweetly, he tried to focus on her face. She was kidding him, right?

"I'm afraid it's true. She will be here in a few days. You can squawk all you want, Mr. Sloan, but the deed is done. You told Ben you would be married and settled down and responsible. Now it's time to prove those words weren't a farce."

"I can't make anyone happy, Miss Adeline. I'll make a bride miserable and what if she," he stopped before spitting out his next words.

"Dies?" she said softly. The woman could certainly read minds. "Then you will have to deal with this, Mr. Sloan. Stop worrying about things that haven't come upon you yet. It's time to move on and I am here to help you." She stood, the conversation over.

"What's her name?" Dawson asked, rising from the chair to follow his hostess to the door.

"Grace Holloway. She'll be here in two days. Pull yourself together until then. Oh, and Mr. Sloan, she's got a degree in accounting. She can do wonders with numbers so my suggestion is to let her get your accounts back in order."

"No kidding? A degree, huh?"

"Yes, Mr. Sloan, a degree that will be applied to your books to get your business flowing again. Oh, and send Lily to me. I have a proposition for her."

Dawson turned and tipped his hat before the door closed. "Thank you, ma'am."

He strolled down the street, never looking across at the saloon or at the others who watched him cross to his office on the corner.

Grace was exhausted. Perhaps a bit happy, too. She was having the best time of her life traveling across the country, grinning from ear to ear when the New York landscape passed her by. In the last few days, she met so many wonderful people and quirky characters, she almost wished she had taken up newspaper writing instead of accounting. The stories that were told on a train were something to capture on paper for sure.

Grace decided to write to a friend of hers who was also struggling in a man's world. Her friend Charity had wanted to become a reporter and was so happy to get the job on the New York Times paper. As it turned out, all the exciting jobs there went to the men. Her friend was only allowed to report on fashion and food. Many times Charity vowed to fight the establishment. Grace smiled at the thought of her friend fighting the big names in journalism. If anyone could do so, it was Charity. She would be the first person to write to. Perhaps she could talk Charity into a westward adventure.

"Next stop, Wichita Falls," the conductor announced. He clasped his hands over his mouth so his voice could be heard all the way back through the passenger train. Before she realized, the train came to a halt, the steady pace of the rail road car no longer moving. This was her stop. Grace reached nervously for her carpetbag, lugging it behind as she moved herself to the front, following the small crowd getting off at Wichita Falls.

Would he be here waiting? Her instructions were from a woman named Adeline Adams, proprietor of the boarding house on Main Street and Ruby's aunt. She instructed Grace to wait at the station until her intended picked her up. Grace hung on to the iron rail as she stepped down from the metal steps of the train. Feeling silly, she hung on to her faded piece of luggage with one hand while swinging back and forth on the edge of the last step, her pointy booted foot moving through the air. A giggle erupted from her mouth and she almost fell off.

"I'll take that from you, ma'am," a deep voice said. When Grace looked up in to the dark eyes of the man standing in front of her, she knew beyond a doubt it was her intended.

A deep flush covered her cheeks when she realized how silly she must look swinging from the rail. "I apologize, sir, that was not very lady-like," Grace muttered, covering a gloved hand over her cheek.

His brow rose as he stared at her for a brief moment. Then he grinned. So she gave him one of her sweetest, biggest smiles and a curtsy. The blue and grey two piece dress she wore had velvet layers and tiny red roses sewed across the hem. She wore red gloves to match that came to her wrists, and a matching hat with a brim wide enough to hide the skin of her porcelain cheeks from the elements.

"You must be Miss Holloway, then?" the man asked. Grace found him rather handsome if she had to say so herself. He was taller, much taller than her five foot five frame and the suit he wore didn't hide the size of his muscles. He had a strong jawline as if he came from a working family. His honey-colored hair was neat and trimmed, a far cry from some of the men who rode the train. When he smiled at her, she was happy to see he had a great set of white teeth. If he was to be her husband, it sure would make it much easier if he had a smile that would be pleasing to look at.

Grace stood there, eyeing him the same as he was doing to her. Just because she was a woman didn't mean she couldn't stare at a man. Besides, this one was about to become her husband. It helped he was sturdy and good to look at. She giggled at her treacherous thoughts then looked away.

"You sure are full of smiles and giggles," he told her. "I'm Dawson Sloan."

"Thank you, Mr. Sloan. I'm pleased to meet you." Her eyes danced with merriment. Grace was indeed happy. This town, the more she glanced around, was a far cry from the streets of New York City. She couldn't wait to have a closer look.

"My pleasure," he said, although a frown began to appear.

"Is something wrong, sir?" she asked. He didn't answer but took her by the elbow and began to help her off the depot platform. They walked along the dusty street until he stopped in front of the parish.

"This is it," he said. "Are you ready to become Mrs. Sloan?"

"Already?" she asked. "I thought I could at least tidy up some. Why, I had no idea I would be whisked off to the alter first thing."

"I didn't have much choice. My house has one bedroom. I can't let you spend the night there unless we are married. It wouldn't be proper and I can't sully your good name. Please, forgive me. It's not my intention to be pushy."

Grace smiled. She knew the real reason why. She was an accountant and if his business was in trouble that meant he didn't have the money to put her up at a boarding house or hotel for a long period of time. Getting married was the only option for a man with money troubles. "I understand. Well, then, Mr. Sloan, let's do this." She held out her arm and began to walk towards the door. He had no choice but to follow along.

Reverend Conners and his wife greeted Grace as if she were a welcoming guest. Their friendly chatter made it easier to get through the ceremony. Afterwards, when Daniel Conners said to kiss the bride, Grace actually took a step forward. She wasn't one to make mountains out of molehills, nope. She usually ploughed through things full speed ahead, worrying about the minuscule things afterwards. Besides, she was anxious to take a look at the business books.

Except the kiss almost floored her and she forgot the reason why she was here in the first place. Dawson stood before her, holding her one hand as the preacher announced, *You may kiss the bride*!

Dawson didn't hesitate at all. He leaned forward and placed his mouth over hers, then pulled her closer as the kiss deepened. Grace's eyes flew open before she slammed them shut when she realized how close he was. She felt his arm across her back and leaned in to the kiss. Her head went back causing her hat to drop to the floor.

The preacher made some strange noises with his throat. Dawson pulled himself away, taking a step back, looking pleasingly surprised. Grace immediately noticed the loss. Goodness, gracious, she'd just been kissed thoroughly by her new husband and she was speechless. Not only was he handsome, he kissed her like she'd never been kissed before.

What a new, wonderful world she was coming into. Grace smiled. "Well, um, that was nice."

"Not bad," Dawson agreed. He grinned and gave her a wink before the preacher had them sign the wedding document.

There was a knock on the door before it opened by a woman in a beautiful, long, blue dress. She held herself in such a regal way, Grace had an idea who she was. Immediately, she went to her. "You must be Miss Adeline, Ruby's aunt," Grace said, holding out her gloved hand.

"Yes, dear. I am and please call me Addie. You are now Grace Sloan, I presume? I apologize for missing the ceremony, I was caught up in a serious ordeal."

Grace realized she was indeed Mrs. Sloan now. "Yes, I am." She kind of liked her new name. It sounded, well, important. Looking around the room at the people there, Grace decided so far she liked this place and the people weren't bad either. She could easily make a home and a name for herself here. After all, she had a degree in accounting. She was certain the business would bloom after she got a hold of things.

"Already thinking of the books, aren't you, dear?" She hadn't realized Miss Adeline had leaned over and spoke for her ears alone.

Grace smiled. "I am," she told her. "I am happy that I decided to come here but now I'm itching to get started. If it weren't for the job offer of looking over the books, I probably wouldn't have gone to all this trouble. It was a long journey."

"Then you must get some rest before anything else." Miss Adeline excused herself and spoke to Dawson quietly. He immediately looked up to stare at her. What was she doing, Grace wondered.

Dawson announced their leaving. "Thank you kindly for the reception, but my new wife has to be exhausted from her journey. We'll take our leave now."

After saying their good-byes, the two left the parish, turning right towards the saloon she could see in the distance. Grace became nervous when she realized they were starting to walk towards the more shady end of town. "Where are we going?" she asked, a bit nervous when one of the cowboys rode by slowly, the clip clop of horse's hooves hitting the dust as he stared at Grace.

"No worries, my place is right on the corner. As long as you don't cross the street, you'll be fine. Stay away from the saloon and no one will bother you."

"Are you sure?" she asked, her voice a bit nervous. She was holding his arm and clung on a bit tighter. New York City had some seedy areas of the city but she knew what parts to avoid, especially at night. To be honest, she never went out alone at night, not if she could help it. Here, with a saloon close by and rowdy cowboys staring her down, Grace wondered how safe this town was.

He reached over and patted her arm. "Don't worry, you're safe with me."

She glanced at him as they walked down the street. He smiled before looking away as she studied his profile. He seemed confident how he held himself and walked like a man with dignity. Yet, there was something about his eyes that bothered her. He had such dark circles underneath, and a sadness that seemed to be buried deep down in a haunted soul. Grace was good at reading people. There was more to this man than anyone realized. As his wife, she assumed it would be her duty to get to the bottom of things.

Several men nodded and tipped their hat to her as they strolled along, taking their time so she could see the town. Dawson pointed out several buildings that the land title company owned. A cabin set back on a side street was built not too long ago. It sat away from the main area. "I like the location of the cabin," she told him.

"It's set back pretty far and that's the way the new occupants like to live. Until the street is built up with other homes, I'm afraid they're all alone on the side street. Most people buy right along main street to be in the thick of things."

"Can we take a look at all the company property?"

"Sure can. Let's get you settled and rested and tomorrow we'll go on a tour of the holdings of Sloan Brothers Land & Title Company."

"Your brother is your partner, I assume?"

He hesitated for a moment. "Yes," Dawson admitted. "He owns the majority share. I have twenty-five percent in the business, he has the rest. Truth be told, Ben isn't happy with me. Land sales have been down and the business is in the red. If I don't bring sales back up, I'm certain he'll close me down." Dawson stopped, turning to her. He took her other arm, a pleading look in his eyes.

Grace was in trouble. He was adorable and so handsome that she wanted to stand on her tip toes and give him a big kiss. But it wasn't appropriate to do so in broad daylight. Instead, she looked up and smiled. "I'm good at accounting. Why not let me take a look at things?"

He stared at her, grinning.

Grace stared right back, a smile upon her own face. "It was one of the reasons why you agreed to marry me, sir. I'm no slouch. I certainly would not have married you if not for the accounting job at hand. So, let's be honest with each other up front and acknowledge that we are both here for one purpose, to make the business a winner and keep your brother from shutting it down."

Such relief shone in his eyes that Grace couldn't help but reach up a hand and rest it on his cheek. As she realized what she did, her hand quickly moved but he caught it first. The warmth from his fingers took her by surprise and she stepped back as if caught unaware. "You have no idea how much those words mean to me," he told her, leaning in closer.

Grace happened to look up to notice a few women standing in front of the mercantile staring open-mouthed at the two of them. She wanted to holler across the street and tell them to watch out before a bug flies in their mouths but she behaved herself. Besides, no lady would act so improper to suggest such a thing.

Dawson followed her line of vision. "We best be moving along, before we tarnish your good reputation," he suggested. He began to walk towards the title company, a small building sitting on the corner of main street and a side street. "This is it, home."

Grace stopped to take a look at her new home. It was as small as a cracker box. How in the world was she going to live there with a man like Dawson Sloan?

Chapter 3

Dawson pulled a set of keys from his pocket as they stepped up on the wooden porch in front of his business. He knew the exact moment she became quiet and grinned to himself. She obviously thought this little abode was their new home. Little did she know the house behind the shop was his also. He was going to have fun with this as long as she didn't get too upset. He needed her. Not even sure why he felt the need to tease her, it just felt good inside. She seemed like such a smart lady who loved to laugh. He liked making her do so.

He flung open the front door as the bell clanged loudly. "Well, what do you think?"

Dawson watched her eyes flicker as they took in the small room. His large desk sat in front of the only window in the room, its bulky wooden frame taking up most of the space. A pot-bellied stove sat in the middle of the floor with an iron bin to keep extra coals, along with a shovel for dishing them in to the stove. The rest of the small room was bare, except for a long bench against a bare wall where guests would sit to wait their turn to see the land agent. The far wall had one long, heavy looking dark curtain from ceiling to floor, where a door was hiding the structure behind the office.

She took a few steps in, looking beyond the pot-bellied stove. "Where do we sleep?" she asked, her voice almost a mere whisper.

"I rarely sleep," he said, humor in his voice, even though he told the truth. Then she looked up at him, those blue eyes sceptical.

A large grin slowly spread across her face. "Mr. Sloan, you are joshing me. I'm certain this is not where we live." She marched over to the dark curtain and pulled it aside. There was another doorway with a paned window filtering in some light. She peeked outside. "Ah ha! I believe you were trying to fool me, sir."

Dawson laughed aloud, surprising himself. It was the the first time in ages he had let loose straight from his gut. He strolled to the door and unlocked it with another key. "Watch your step." Through the door and down the two steps, they went back up two other steps before he unlocked yet another door. "This is your new home."

He grinned when she turned to him, her mouth opened wide.

"It's nothing like I imagined," she told him, shock still all over her beautiful face. She was so lovely and when she smiled like that, Dawson ached to pull her in his arms. He had been missing something in his life and it turned out to be companionship.

Dawson shook himself. He had to remember he didn't deserve to be happy or to have someone look at him like she was doing. For a few moments, he almost forgot about the tragedy. He couldn't ever forget, it wouldn't be right. Not when the whole family suffered such a horrific loss and it was still his fault. He had no right to be happy. Ever. It was best to remember that and forget about a relationship with someone. He put the suitcase down and turned to leave. "I'll be in the office, there are several things I need to do," he said in a brisk, rough voice, then left her standing in the middle of the room.

The surprised look on her face bothered him immensely, yet he couldn't help himself. He didn't deserve to enjoy himself and laughing again felt so good and yet reminded him he had no right to do so.

<> <>

Grace had never been in such a lovely home before. A dark, heavy wooden table was sitting in the center of the large kitchen with several high-backed chairs and two benches tucked up tight against the table. A beautiful linen tablecloth made of lace covered the top, and a glass vase with wilted flowers sat in the middle. Grace's first thought was to find some fresh flowers to replace the wilted ones. A large modern cook stove sat in the far corner of the room, along with several pieces of wood shelving, stocked with various items.

Working her way to the next room, Grace was amazed at the trinkets on various antique tables and several cushioned seating areas. In the parlor was a beautiful Victorian carved walnut set of chairs and a settee, along with several oil paintings hung on one wall. Immediately, her accountant's eye began to add up the wealth in the rooms. If his business was in dire

straits, selling off some of these items may be the answer to his problems. Grace wondered why he hadn't thought of this before.

First, she'd have to see the books and all his holdings. A spry in her step at the challenge ahead had Grace picking out the most expensive pieces. Where in the world did a land title agent get all these fine pieces of furniture?

A solid oak door off the parlor called to her. Grace turned the cold knob to find a beautiful French Henri II queen bed, the coverlet hand-quilted in beautiful shades of material that dropped her jaw open wide. She let her fingers run over the beautiful hand-carved designs on the headboard. An old Mahogany Province armoire sat against the one wall, along with a carved wooden padded chair. On the other side of the room was a fireplace, a rocker tucked close by. Grace imaged herself lying in this bed on a cold winter's night, the fire crackling and warming the big room.

Her mind imagined her new husband curled up with her, his arms around her as they stared in to the fire, romantic flames flickering in a darkened room. Slowly, Grace lowered herself to the bed, curling on her side as she slid in to oblivion dreaming about her new life and husband.

<> <>

Grace woke with a start. A small wool blanket was draped over her shoulders. She blinked her eyes several times to see her husband pick up a fire iron to push the lit embers around. After some time, flames flickered, shadowing his profile as he bent down in front of the fireplace. She watched quietly as he removed his jacket, setting it over a hook on the back of the door. He loosened the top buttons of his shirt, pulling the tail from his waist and stretching his arms out in front of him before lowering himself to the rocker close by.

A surge of fear engulfed Grace. It was their marriage night. Would he demand his rights tonight? She wasn't even sure how she felt about this new position she found herself in. Married to a man who was incredibly handsome and yet neither one wanted a real marriage. He wanted her to fix his business and she was itching to get her hands on him, er, his books. When he turned his head, she slammed her eyes shut, praying he hadn't noticed she stared so. She heard him sigh. It was a tired sigh, as if he was too exhausted to move from his spot.

A few minutes went by so Grace peeked to find his eyes closed, his long lashes lowered against his rough skin. He lifted a hand in his sleep and rubbed his clean shaven jaw before letting his hand drop to his lap. Grace sighed. She watched him as he slept, wondering if he would indeed come to bed. She wasn't sure what she would do if he did. Her eyes drooped as she fell asleep once again watching him as he rested.

Something woke her up. Grace pushed herself from the bed to find the rocker empty. She shook the wool blanket from her shoulders and followed the noise she heard near the kitchen. The back door closed quietly. Frowning, Grace noticed her luggage was still by the door. She picked up her carpet bag to shift through her belongings, finding a shawl to throw over her shoulders.

It was dark outside, the streets quiet. Grace had no idea why he left but she wanted to know why he would go somewhere on his wedding night. Oh, she knew it wasn't a real wedding, but for a man to leave his bride was confusing. She took the few steps to the office and turned the knob. It was open. Good, he was concerned about his work and decided to stay up late and work on his business. Grace would offer to help now. There was no sense going back to bed since she had a hearty nap.

The office was empty. Grace saw a shadow outside and made her way to the front door. She opened the door, the bell jangling. "Shh," she told the door, then giggled when she realized she was talking to an inanimate object. She didn't have to worry, Dawson never heard or looked back. His determined steps crossing the street made Grace believe he was on a mission.

The saloon was lively this time of night. She heard the sounds of a piano in the night, clapping and stomping faintly in the background. Dawson strolled down the street, weaving his way towards the saloon doors. He hadn't put on his jacket, his shirt tail hanging out. Grace pulled her shawl tighter. Was he going to the saloon? Why? He had told her to stay away from that area and now here he was, heading straight towards the forbidden doors.

A commotion began inside right before two men stumbled out. They almost fell over the porch, weaving their way around Dawson as he walked right through the door.

Grace wasn't sure what to make of this. Was he a drinking man? If so, she wouldn't abide this. Her hands went to grab her shawl a little tighter. The cool night was a bit chilly so she waited a few more minutes and when he didn't return, she turned on her heels and went back inside the office. She didn't care how much noise the bell above the door frame made.

Feeling her way around the large desk, she found a wooden match and lit the oil lamp. Turning it up so she could see, Grace sat down on the high-back chair. She may as well get started. It was time to find out just how deep in debt Mr. Sloan was. Things didn't look good at all. No, siree, she worried her bottom lip, this was looking bad if he was going to gamble his money away. Is that what he was doing at the saloon? She found his ledgers in the top left drawer and opened the first one.

Rubbing her eyes, Grace got up several times to stir the coals in the stove. In the early morning hours before daylight, it seemed to be the coolest. Grace was exhausted but wanted to finish what she started. Several times, she stood on the front porch, gazing over to the saloon but the lights were still on there, although the world outside had gone quiet. It didn't look as if many customers were there any longer. She wondered how long he would be? The piano music had stopped hours ago. Grace heard an occasional shout from inside but when Dawson didn't emerge from the saloon, she closed her eyes and leaned on the post along the porch. Was he going to leave her every night for whatever was going on there?

With a sigh, Grace went back inside, determined to finish at least the first ledger. So far, the books looked fine. Everything was accounted for and he seemed to know what he was doing. Then why was he in trouble? Perhaps it wasn't the books but his holdings. How much property did he actually own? How much had he sold recently? Mayhaps he was hanging on to too much property. She'd get to the bottom of things. With a yawn, Grace stood up and stretched. It had been a long night.

Looking back once more, she saw the last light go out in the saloon. It wasn't quite sunrise yet, so Grace went back outside to stand on the porch and wait for him to come back. After ten minutes and no sign of Dawson, a frown appeared. Where in tar-nation was he? There was a small bench against the wall right under the window. She sat down and waited since Grace didn't want to go back in the house alone just yet.

Grace's eyes were getting heavy when she heard a noise across the street. The saloon door creaked as it opened when Dawson walked out, stretching his arms in front of him. She almost smiled until a woman walked out behind him. Grace watched as she placed a hand on his upper arm. He turned to her before placing his own hand on her shoulder, patting it gently as if he were familiar with her. It appeared as if they were talking to each other before the woman turned and went back inside. Grace didn't get a good look at the lady, except she wore a long, dark skirt that swished back and forth when she moved. She hadn't looked cheap like those painted ladies in the penny novels she had read about. Her hair was pulled back, not all fancied up and her clothes were proper.

She tried to remember her mother's wise words that some things are not always how they appear and yet, Dawson was a married man who spent the night not with his wife but with another woman in a saloon.

Grace's world was crashing down right in front of her. She stood up, anger beginning to encompass her whole body. How dare he make a fool of her, mail order bride or not! She may have fallen in to this without realizing what was happening at the time but that didn't give him the right to flaunt a fancy lady in front of her and the whole town.

Dawson's hair was tussled and he strolled across the street as if it didn't matter that he was coming home before the sun was up. Was it acceptable to the town for a man to behave this way here? Did he not think anything of the way he behaved?

He didn't seem to notice her at first, his head was down and he looked exhausted. Grace pursed her lips and crossed the shawl tighter around her shoulders. She stood on the wooden porch blocking the door. When Dawson looked up and saw her standing there, he skidded to a stop, then slowly made his way towards her, taking long strides until he stood in front of her.

The two of them looked at each other in silence. "It isn't what you think," Dawson told her, his voice rough as if it was hard for him to speak. She stared in to his eyes, they looked haunted, wild, as if he had been going through something awful.

"Are you alright?" she asked, angry but worried there was more to this than meets the eye.

"I will be once I start the day."

"Have you slept?" she asked him, her voice angry but concerned.

He placed a hand on her elbow to steer her inside. When the bell jangled, she walked in, Dawson behind her. The door went shut and she turned to face him, prepared to let him have a piece of her mind. "I'm not sure how things are done out here, but I have no intention of being a placid wife. I won't sit idly by while you tally with saloon girls and drink your problems away."

He shrugged. "I didn't have a drink tonight. You sound like the rest of them."

"The rest of who?" She turned away, afraid of the look on his face. He was a haunted man, it was clear to see but she wasn't about to go down that road with him. He had no right to treat her like this on her wedding night.

"My friends. They think I need to clean up my act but no one has any idea what I have to deal with every single night."

Grace swung around. "Why don't you tell me, after all, I am your wife now. I told you, I won't stand for this."

It was clear the man had demons. He gritted his teeth and said, "I don't have to tell you that you are here because of my business. You have a degree in accounting. It doesn't take an expert to know you didn't come here for me."

He was right. Had she known how handsome he was going to be, she may have thought twice. The part about having feelings for someone didn't abode well with her. She wanted to work on books and ledgers, not on a marriage. But she was here. "I'm sorry you feel that way, Dawson. I am trying to make the best of things but I've been here barely twenty four hours and look what you've done!"

Dawson sighed. He took a chair at the desk. "I know, I'm sorry. It's not what you think, I promise, but I can't discuss this with you right now." He brought his head up, looking in to her eyes. "Please, trust me."

She worked her way to his side and knelt down. Taking his face in her hands, she almost backed away at the touch of his warm skin. But she held fast. "I want to help you, Dawson. I am good at accounting. Marriage, not so much. It is all new to me but I won't stand for a husband to flaunt himself in a saloon as if I mean nothing."

He raised his hands and placed them over hers. She almost jumped back at his touch. His hands were so warm and even though calloused from hard work, they felt nice on her skin. She almost closed her eyes and leaned in. Almost. If he was trying to soften the blow by being kind, he had another think coming. Grace needed to stay angry or he would continue the behavior she saw tonight. "I can't let you make a fool of me, Dawson Sloan."

"I promise I won't."

"Then don't go back there again." She realized the moment she spoke those words she had said the wrong thing. His hands left her and he pushed back the chair.

When he stood up, Grace was still kneeling by the chair. He looked so tall and formidable. A tortured man stood before her, and she wanted to know why. "I don't know if I can keep that promise, Grace."

"You have to. Who is the woman?"

Dawson took a step to the window. He ran a hand over his hair and sighed. "Her name is Lily. She isn't who you may think. Lily is a friend, that's all. She's helped me with the nightmares."

Grace crossed her arms over her bodice. "Do you think I'm daft? You ask me to trust you, after you've been dallying with a woman all night, in a saloon, I may add. How do you think it looks from where I am standing?"

"I know, it looks bad. I'm sorry. I didn't want to wake you."

Grace tapped her toe on the wooden floor, frustrated. "You are a married man now. I am not sure what is the truth and what isn't but believe me, I'll get to the bottom of things. Just like I do with the accounts. Mr. Sloan, I forbid you to dally with that woman as long as we are married."

Dawson turned to stare at her. She was serious and stared right back at him. She hadn't come all this way to be made a fool of. Most women didn't talk back to their husbands but she wasn't most.

He grinned. "Mrs. Sloan, you are adorable when angry."

His smile was catching. She grinned right back. "You haven't seen anything yet, Mr. Sloan."

He took a few steps toward her, stopping about an inch away. Grace held her breath. Dawson lifted his hand and cupped her chin. "I promise," he said, his voice low and husky, "I won't dally with Lily again. I'll go tell her so right now."

Grace stood frozen to the wooden floor as the door slammed shut, the bell jingling in the background. He was going back to tell her so? That made no sense. She began walking towards the door to call him back when his words earlier hit her.

She's helped me with the nightmares. "What nightmares?" What exactly was Grace getting in to here.

Chapter 4

After Dawson left, Grace decided to clean up and go to the mercantile. Since she was going to be working in the small office, it needed some sprucing up. She lugged a small table from the house to the office and set it in front of the long wooden bench. All it needed was a small vase of flowers, a dish with candies and perhaps a few books to make the room a bit more cozy. On a mission, Grace left the land office and began her trek towards the mercantile. She steered clear of the saloon, the structure appearing too quiet this time of morning.

A few men walked down the boarded walk, nodding to her and tipping their hats. "Good morning, gentlemen," she offered to three men strolling by.

She entered the mercantile. "Ma'am, I'll be with you shortly," a voice called out.

"I'm in no hurry," Grace told the older man. "I'll look around." She wandered through the two isles of merchandise, picking out what she needed while the owner of the store took care of his customer. As Grace got closer to them, she noticed a well-dressed lady at the counter.

The woman turned to her and smiled, holding out her hand. "Good morning, Mrs. Sloan. Nice to meet you again. We met briefly at the wedding ceremony."

Grace took her hand, remembering. Right now, she wasn't in a mood to recall yesterday's wedding. "Good morning, Miss Addie. Nice to see you again, too."

"Would you care to have tea? I have some steeping on the stove as we speak. It's just a walk down the block."

Grace nodded. It would be nice to talk to another woman. "Sure, I need a few things and I'll be along."

"I'll wait. We'll walk together." Miss Addie stepped to the side while Grace paid for her purchases from the money she brought with her. She tried to pick up the penny novel and other things from the counter but the owner stopped her.

"Nonsense, Mrs. Sloan. I'll have these things delivered to your house this afternoon. Little Billy is coming in today to work off a train set he wanted some time back. If I don't give him chores to do, he'll be under my feet, asking me a million questions I can't answer."

"Very well, thank you, sir."

"Names Jimmy, not sir."

"Thank you, Jimmy." Grace walked down the street with Miss Addie towards a lovely home set between the parish and a row of three empty houses, where pretty flowers graced the porch in wooden-like boxes. A sign hung over her porch, Miss Adeline's Boarding House.

Grace followed her inside to find a homey atmosphere. She felt welcomed the moment she stepped inside the parlor. "What a lovely place," Grace told her new friend.

"I've worked hard to make it so, thank you. Now, Grace, if I may call you Grace?" At her nod, Addie went on. "Sit right down and I'll get our tea."

A few moments later, Miss Addie came in carrying a silver tray with two porcelain cups, along with a sugar bowl and tiny creamer set. As they busied themselves with making the tea, Grace waited for Miss Addie's questions. It was why she was invited here, she was certain. Not one for small talk, Grace decided to get down to business. After all, she was an accountant and timing was everything. "Miss Addie, thank you for inviting me. I'm sure you have some things to tell me and it's why I'm here. I don't dally so talk away."

Miss Addie put down her cup. "I like you, young lady. You are right, I do have some things to say. However, I like to meet the ladies that have taken it upon themselves to take up my offer of becoming a mail order bride. I've screened you myself as I do each and every single person on my list. Those who want to be a bride and the men who need a bride. No one gets past my scrutiny. Saying that, I know Mr. Sloan is going through some difficult times at the moment and I am hoping you will understand if he has a slow start with this marriage. He is a fine man otherwise. I would not have him on my list if it weren't the truth."

Grace knew he was hiding something. Maybe now she would find out what. "What happened to him, Miss Addie?"

The older woman seemed hesitant to speak. She picked up her teacup again and sipped slowly. At first Grace didn't think she would answer but then she did. "He has awful nightmares of the attack that happened some time ago down by the creek property. Two children died there and he blames himself even though he didn't have a hand in the murders. Outlaws tried to oust a family that bought the property from Sloan Brothers Land and Title Company."

A hand went to Grace's mouth. "That's terrible," she whispered, shocked at the news.

"I don't normally tell other people's business affairs but you are his wife and he needs you, Grace. I am hoping you can calm his tortured demons and make him realize it wasn't his fault."

"What happened? Tell me, please," she asked, wanting to know all the details so she could help her husband.

Miss Addie went on. "Dawson had hired a young man, one of the Murphy boys, to be an apprentice. He had taught the young man how to sell property and the boy did great. Then Dawson got notice a shipment of his parents furniture was waiting for him. So he left for Fort Worth for a few days and told the Murphy boy he was in charge. Dawson thought for a few days the boy would be able to handle the shop. That's how it all started."

Grace's heart began to pound. "What did he do?"

"There have been outlaw sightings down by a certain section of the river recently. A few years ago a man built a cabin there but then sold it back to Dawson last year when the outlaws began to pester him. When Dawson realized how dangerous it was in that location, he agreed to give the man his money back and sold him something else in a safer area. He was going to tear the cabin down and leave the land barren but hadn't done so yet. Dawson left clear instructions to the young man the cabin was not to be sold."

A gut-wrenching feeling came upon Grace. "The boy sold the land, didn't he?"

"Yes, while Dawson was away. He wanted to sell as much land as he could and try to impress Dawson. The family who wanted it, loved the area and insisted on buying it, so the Murphy boy gave in. When Dawson came back and found out it was sold, he tried to tell the family it was a mistake but the new owner refused to leave. He wouldn't let Dawson buy it back. Your husband went every single day to convince him otherwise, to no avail." Addie took a sip of her tea. "I'm sorry, this is difficult but I must tell you. I'm afraid Dawson will never do so."

Grace was feeling sick to her stomach. She placed the tea cup on the table. "Go on." She had to hear the rest no matter how horrible.

"Dawson was heading there one morning like he always did when he heard screams. Two outlaws were attacking the family. The father was trying to save his daughters, two young girls no more than ten years old, but one of the outlaws pistol whipped him, knocking him out cold. When Dawson came upon them, he shot both outlaws dead. But it didn't bring back the girls."

Grace began to cry. She let the tears fall. How awful to come upon such a scene. "How long ago did this happen?"

"A bit over six months ago."

"Long enough to put his business in jeopardy." It was no wonder he was falling behind. If he hadn't had a sale in six months, it could ruin him. She began to feel empathy towards her husband and his nightmares.

"He needs you, Grace. It may be why you are here."

Grace smiled at her new friend. Miss Addie could be misconstrued as a busy body but she had the best intentions. She cared about this town and all its inhabitants. Someone had to. The west was not a friendly place.

"Is that why he left me last night on our wedding night? The nightmares get the best of him? Is it why he was in the arms of Lily?" Grace hated to mention the other woman because it still made her angry. Being in another person's arms no matter what happened was wrong. She did remember Dawson telling her to trust him. It wasn't what she thought. Now she understood more.

She thought she'd get a shocked reaction from Addie but was wrong on all accounts. Miss Addie smiled. "Lily's heart is already taken, Grace. She's head over heels in love with Dawson's brother, Ben."

"Oh, my! Then why would he run to her when he has a wife at home? I am puzzled by this whole affair."

Miss Addie patted her hand. "No need to be. He can't be alone. She had reached out to him one night when he was walking the streets up and down, hour after hour. They made a deal but you have to talk to him about that. I'm not certain of the details."

Grace stood. "Thank you for telling me this. Not to be rude, but I must take my leave. It looks like my new found freedom has its limits. I have work to do on not only my accounting skills but my marriage as well. Good day, Miss Addie."

When Grace returned to the office, as promised, her package was waiting by the door. She noticed a small boy work his way past her as she was coming down the boarded walk. She turned to thank him but he had zig-zagged his way through the others behind her and disappeared into what seemed like thin air. A smile crossed her face right before she pushed open the door.

The jingle of the bell didn't capture Dawson's attention, who was sitting at his desk going over some paperwork. He looked exhausted but content, never even looking up to see who entered. She had to fix him and she'd find a way to do so, by the grace of God, she would.

Grace sat on the bench while she opened her package. Inside were two penny novels she had chosen from the mercantile. She laid them out on the table as if on display, along with the medium size copper dish she bought. Digging into the wrapping paper, she pulled out a small cloth bag filled with hard candies. They made a noise as she unwrapped the twine and poured the candy into the dish. She was concentrating so much she didn't see the hand snake out and grab one of the candies. A smile played on her lips as she looked up to see Dawson pop the candy in his mouth.

"Spending my hard-earned money already, wife?" he teased.

She shook her head. "No. Mine. I had a job at the Montgomery Wards before coming out here. I've got plenty of savings. How does it look?" she asked, pointing to the new arrangement.

"Looks fine, Grace. Thank you."

Grace cocked her head to the side. "Your welcome, but I'm not sure why."

"For trying to make things look nice here. I didn't see the need but I've been wrong about many things. I appreciate you trying."

Grace took his hands in hers. "You, sir, are welcome. Now, let's close this place down. We have a ton of work to do."

He stepped back. "I can't close here. What if -"

She shook her head. "I want you to show me everything Sloan Brothers owns. It shouldn't take too long."

"Right now?"

She nodded. "We may as well get started right away. No sense putting it off. From what I understand, your brother will be here in less than a month."

Dawson agreed. He took her by the elbow and steered her through the door after flipping the open sign to closed. As they walked down the street, Grace listened to him talk about the properties he owned. He was in his element, his face lit up as he spoke. She smiled, knowing how much he loved the kind of work he did. The two of them would get along great.

They crossed the street, walking towards the parish. After passing Miss Adeline's boarding house, Dawson stopped. "These three houses you see right here are owned by our company."

"May we look inside?"

"Certainly. All three are identical, so you would only need to take a look at the first one." Dawson unlocked while Grace toured the first home, walking through each small room. Satisfied, she turned around so quickly she landed up against him, not realizing how close he had been. Dawson's arms shot out.

"I'm sorry," he said before placing a kiss on her mouth. It was quick and startled her.

She pulled back, surprised at his kiss. Then she wrapped her arms around his neck and pulled him in for another of those sweet kisses. The surprised look on Dawson's face when she kissed him made her giggle. Yet, he was quick to react when he wrapped his arms around her waist and began to hum as his feet moved and he began to dance, swaying them back and forth. Then he took her arm and twirled her around the empty room. By now, Grace was laughing out loud, a slight rise in her voice when he ended their dance with a dip as she flung backwards, her head and neck straining towards the floor.

He pulled her upright and bowed. "My lady," he teased, laughter in his voice.

Grace gave him a hug. "That was nice, thank you. We best keep moving along," she told him, pulling him towards the door.

The moment a child's voice called out to his mother down the street, Grace saw the instant change in Dawson. His steps became harsher, he became quiet and sullen, angry even. There was no longer any teasing as they went through the inventory on each street. Grace didn't want him to know she already knew why. Not yet. He was starting to relax. Afraid he would turn away, she was glad for at least his hand still at her elbow as they walked. Even though Miss Addie said Lily was in love with someone else, she didn't want her husband going to that woman for comfort. She wanted him to come to her.

When they got back to the office, Grace turned to Dawson. "How long has the three houses been sitting empty?"

He shrugged. "I don't rightly know. Perhaps, six months or so."

"What I thought."

"What do you mean?" he asked, a suspicious look beginning to appear on his face.

Grace noticed any time she mentioned anything, no matter what, about the time period of six months ago, he tightened up, his voice became harsh and he collapsed within himself. This could not go on any longer. She would fix his books and him, as soon as she figured out how. The books, now that was no longer a problem. She knew exactly what she could do to get those homes sold.

But, Dawson, that was a whole new thing for her. She didn't have a degree in managing men.

Grace sighed, pacing back and forth in the small office. She placed her hands behind her back and turned to him. "I have a great idea for getting those three homes sold. Let's open them to the public, for one day only, invite the town, have refreshments and give them a tour. Perhaps someone's relative may be interested, or may know someone who is in want of a house. Who knows, perhaps someone may buy it that very day."

"You mean like an open house to the public?" When she nodded, he rubbed his jaw. "That may work." He grinned. "By George, Mrs. Sloan, I think you have something here."

A smile graced her cheeks. "Now, tell me, Mr. Sloan, who is the richest in the territory? I want to make sure to send an invitation and invite all their friends."

Chapter 5

The day with Grace had been exhausting but fun. Dawson had never experienced a woman quite like her before. She knew exactly how she wanted things done. The idea of a public open house to sell their homes was a brilliant idea. She suggested inviting all the townsfolk and others in the surrounding territories to take a look at what they had for sale. She even decided to invite some of the rich landowners from the area. She spent the day writing a letter to each of the five biggest and wealthiest land owners, inviting them to come take a look at these properties. They would make good investments, she told them in her letters, suggesting the ranchers would make the initial investment and rent them out to families or folks who were starting out in this area. It was a perfect idea and he was glad she was here to help.

Dawson had been afraid his brother was going to shut him down. Now that Grace was here, full of ideas that he hoped would work, perhaps Ben would show mercy and hold off for awhile.

Satisfied, he stood over her for a moment as she lay sleeping in the bed. He wasn't sure what to do. If he crawled in along side of her, sooner or later he'd wake her with his nightmares. They were sure to come, they did every single night. He wished now they would go away, even if he deserved to have them. When would the torture end, he wondered, sitting on the rocker by the fireplace.

By this time of night any other evening, he'd high-tail it over to Lily as she got off shift and drink until he staggered to her room. Then they would talk until he fell asleep, and the nightmares would happen. She'd wake him up, over and over, all through the night until early morning. Thinking he'd be feeling tortured and want to run to Lily for the usual comfort, he didn't have an inkling of desire to go now. He had told Lily earlier that he wouldn't be back, even tried giving cash to tide her over until she left but Lily refused the money like he knew she would.

He glanced at Grace, liking the idea of a wife in the bed next to him. If he could force himself to stay awake all night, there would be no nightmares and perhaps someday he could share her bed.

Dawson rocked slowly, staring into the fire, the motion lulling him to nod off. It wasn't long until the horror began. He was in the middle of the property by the creek, running towards the cabin. He heard voices on the other side but he couldn't break the door down. Hands kept pulling him back from behind but when he tried to turn to see who was grabbing at him, the faces were blank. As he banged on the door, his hands became bloody. He heard the shotgun blasts over and over again as screams began to engulf his ears. Then the fire started as flames shot up, the crackling sounding like dynamite in his ears. He took his bloody hands and covered his ears all the while ghost hands pulled him back from the door. He let them carry him back in to the tall prairie grass, while the cabin became a red glow, its flames shooting up in to the dark night, so high they looked as if they would touch the stars.

The silence was worse then the screaming because he knew everyone inside was dead. Because of him. They all were tortured and burnt. Dawson tried to call out, his voice so hoarse from yelling. He lashed out at the demons behind him, pushing them away.

"Dawson, wake up."

A woman's voice shook some sense into him. His mind told him it must be Lily, his friend who always woke him up every night when he fell asleep after hours of restlessness. Yet, the far away voice calling his name didn't sound like her. As his eyes slowly opened, he realized he was on the rocker, in his own bedroom, in front of the blazing fire in the pit.

"Grace?" he tried to say her name but he was so hoarse he didn't even recognize the sound of his own voice. Dazed, he looked down to see her long, slim fingers prying his own fingers from the death grip he had on the arms of the rocker.

"Dawson, come to bed. Please," she begged him. Actually, it sounded more like an order. He rose out of the chair, too weak to argue as she pulled on the jacket he hadn't taken off earlier. As if mesmerized, he let her undress him. Her soft, gentle fingers opened two buttons at his neck. He stared, in a daze, the memory of the nightmare so vivid in his mind he couldn't think of anything else. It was as if the whole thing was going to start all over again.

When she led him to the bed and pulled the covers down, he sat on the mattress, unable to move. Grace bent down, pulling off his boots then lifting his legs onto the bed. He was still dressed in his britches and shirt but he didn't care. Fatigue whipped at him like a tornado crossing the prairie. Dawson laid his head on the pillow, staring blankly at the ceiling. The flames from the cabin were so vivid in his mind's eye, he shook his head back and forth, silently begging it to stop.

He felt her join him in bed. One arm went under his neck and shoulder and the other wrapped itself around his chest, cradling him in her arms. She held him, her hand stroking his hair, the gentle touch calming his wild-beating heart. His breathing began to steady. Her touch was amazing. It was nothing like Lily, who woke him with words, shaking him so he'd come out of his nightmare. Then they would talk in to the long hours of the night so he didn't fall back to sleep. He'd leave when the sun was about to rise and start his day, too exhausted to get much of anything done. It was one of the reasons his Company was in such dire straits.

Dawson sighed. He tried to raise his hand to touch her, wanting to hold her even more than she was holding him. But she refused, without words, a silent unspoken language between them. Her hand gently stroked his arm, mesmerizing him as he drifted slowly off to sleep.

<> <>

Dawson opened his eyes to find daylight peeking in the windows. The curtains in the bedroom were wide open. A metal tub sat in the middle of the room, steam rising above the metal rim. He heard her humming as she fixed fresh clothes from the wardrobe in the corner of the room.

Sighing deeply, Dawson slowly sat up, stretching his arms in front of him.

"Good morning, sunshine," Grace teased, whipping her skirts around and coming towards him with a skip in her step. She smiled at him as if he were a visitor come calling.

"Grace." He raked his hand through his hair, embarrassed that she had caught him in the middle of a nightmare. "I'm sorry you had to see me like this. Now you know my secrets."

"Nonsense." She kneeled down in front of him, her eyes level with his. "We are in this together. Once you learn I am your wife and my duty is to you, those nightmares will cease. I promise I'll help get you through this."

He took her hand in his, the softness bringing back memories of her touch. "Thank you, Grace. Your mother sure named you right."

She smiled, her beautiful face glowing with happiness. She should be exhausted, having to put up with his sleeplessness and yet here she was, a picture perfect lady with more energy than he could seem to muster up. She pulled at his arms, forcing him from the bed. "Off with you, sir. I have a hot bath awaiting." She moved in the direction of the metal tub.

"Just had a bath the other day," he mumbled, yet looking at the steaming water with a joy leaping in his heart.

"It will relax your strained muscles and make you feel better. Besides, we have a lot of work to do until the open house on Saturday afternoon. I'll be expecting a large crowd." Grace bent down by the fireplace, attempting to pick up another metal pot filled with steaming water.

Dawson quickly made it to her side. "I'll take care of that." He reached over, taking it from her hands. "I don't like that you worked so hard, but thank you."

Grace smiled, lowering her eyes as if embarrassed at his words. "I better leave you to your bath," she said softly, turning towards the door. She slipped out like a ghost in the night. Dawson noticed the rumpled cover on their bed. After she had held him in her arms, he had slept like a baby. Several times he awoke through the night but her arms had been there, gently stroking his skin as she spoke soft words of encouragement. It lulled him back to sleep without any more nightmares.

Dawson lowered himself in to the hot water. Gritting his teeth, the heat began to relax his muscles almost instantly. She was a godsend, knowing what he needed. Leaning back against the tub, he closed his eyes and fell asleep, a smile on his face as he began to dream of his new bride.

<> <>

Grace put the finishing touch on the table when she heard the bedroom door open. "Breakfast at your service, Mr. Sloan," she said, grinning. Her mood was perky today, glad he had entrusted her last night instead of running across the street to the saloon. It was a start now that she understood he wasn't visiting another woman but trying to free his tortured soul.

Well, she would help him with that problem. But right now, there was the matter of the open houses on Saturday. She'd have to push herself and make some urgent demands to get accomplished everything she planned for the success of their venture. After serving flapjacks and warm syrup, Grace sat across from Dawson at their wooden table.

She picked up her fork. "I have a favor to ask and if you say no, it will be fine, except it may turn in to a problem for Saturday."

Dawson's brow rose. He continued to eat the flapjacks as if he hadn't eaten in ages. Swallowing, he finally looked up. "How so?"

Grace put down her fork, not interest in eating at the moment. "We have to decorate one of the houses we will be showing."

"That may be rather expensive. I doubt there's enough in the budget to buy new furniture and décor. Not even sure the mercantile will have what we need," he said between bites.

"I know. I looked at your first ledger. You've been taking good care of the books and you are right. There isn't enough money in your budget to cover what I have in mind. But you have all you need right here." She pointed in the air.

He stopped chewing and looked around. "My parent's furniture?" he said incredulously as if he were affronted of the thought.

Grace saw the surprise and disbelief on his face. She had to tread carefully, now that she realized these things were most likely the furniture he brought back from Fort Worth the day of the tragedy. "We would borrow some things to stage one of the homes.

Make it look comfortable and homey so it appeals to a new customer."

Dawson stared at her before he looked around the kitchen. He nodded after a bout of silence. "This house is filled up with their furniture. I made three trips in the last year," he told her. "I rented a barn in Fort Worth until I could get it all here. Wasn't sure what to do with all of their things after the sale of their ranch."

"How long has it been since they are gone?" she asked, careful not to lose him. He seemed to be opening up and sharing personal thoughts with her for the time being.

"Years, since I was ten."

Grace's mouth fell open. "You've had these things stored for that long?"

"No, of course not. My brother Ben lived in the family home, we had a large spread near Dallas, a fine ranch house. He took over when they died, put me through surveying school and the first chance I had, I got a job on the rail road. My parents loved their home but it wasn't the same without them. Ben joined me here for about a year but then went back to Dallas to sell the ranch. It was time. He's thinking of joining me again, not really sure yet what his intentions are."

"I understand. Let me ask you this. Do you mind if we use the furniture for the open house? I don't want to upset you, after all, they are your parent's things."

"I don't mind. Not really. The house is rather stuffed with a lot, I have to admit." He gave her a smile that melted her heart. Her husband had been through so much tragedy in his youth and now this horrible murder he witnessed. It was no wonder his head was filled with recurring nightmares.

She stood up. "I have no idea what you have dealt with, Dawson, but I want to help you if I can. Please, let me."

He rose. Took both her hands in his. "Now don't you worry about me, Grace. I'll be fine."

"You weren't fine last night. If I recall, you needed me."

A flash of memory shone in his eyes. At first she thought he would be angry at her rash words, but a smile began to play on his face. He tilted his head and kissed her on the cheek. "I do need you, Grace Sloan. More than you can imagine."

At first, the shouting from the street was minimal until a gun went off. Grace ran through the kitchen door, then through the office to the big window to see what was going on, Dawson right behind her. He instantly ran to the desk, opened a drawer and pulled out a pistol before joining her at the window.

Two women stood outside the saloon, screaming at each other. Grace recognized Lily. She had a small pistol in her hand that pointed towards the ground. A bit of smoke expelled from the tip, making Grace realize she had shot it at some point. "Next one goes in your foot," Lily shouted. "Now get my things right now! I'm not leaving without them!"

The older woman, who wore a long skirt with a tight bodice that was terribly revealing, backed up through the doors of the saloon. Grace stood along side of Dawson, staring through the window pane, waiting to see what happened next. "Is it always this exciting in Wichita Falls?" she asked.

"This is the most excitement we've had in months," he said, then realized his chosen words. Grace felt him stiffen immediately. Sure he was recalling the murder at the creek, she reached out and took his hand, not saying a word. At first, he ignored her until she felt warm fingers press into her own. She leaned over and kissed his cheek. "Thank you," she whispered.

Not taking his eyes from the action at the saloon, he whispered back, "What for?"

Grace shrugged. "I don't know. Perhaps for sharing your life with me."

Dawson squeezed her hand. "You are welcome, then."

A suitcase came flying out of the saloon doors, shedding its contents all over the ground. "Now don't come back, ever!" the woman in the saloon shouted.

"We should go help," Grace mentioned.

"No need. Help is on its way."

A wagon came to a stop in front of the saloon, blocking out the view of Lily picking up the scattered garments. Lily placed her belongings in the back of the wagon before climbing up with Miss Addie before it took off down the street.

"We should get started on our day," Grace told her husband, trying to pull her hand from his.

"We should," he agreed, but didn't let go of her hand.

Grace didn't move. She stayed right there, watching the stirring of the small town through the big picture window, happy and content.

"I'm glad you came."

Grace smiled. "So am I."

Chapter 6

"I need to pen a letter to my brother," he told her.

"How long will that take, Dawson?" she asked. "We need to start moving this furniture if we want to stage a grand opening on Saturday."

"Do not worry, I'm going to the post office first, then I will hire some help. You pick out what you would like to use. When I return, we'll get started."

Things were getting better. Grace went about choosing which pieces would look best, noticing they were all elegant and expensive. His parents had to have been well off. Why then, she wondered, was he struggling so while it seemed his brother Ben was the one with all the money? Perhaps there was more to this than she realized.

It was shortly after that Dawson returned, alone.

"Where is the hired help?"

"They'll be here in twenty minutes. We need to talk."

Grace stopped what she was doing and turned to him.

"Come here, Grace." He reached for her hand and guided her to a small settee in the parlor. Sitting beside her, he turned and looked at her with a pained face.

She placed a hand over his cheek. "What is it? What's wrong?"

With a deep sigh, Dawson picked up her hands while he kissed the back of each one. "Grace, you are indeed a godsend. I want you to know the whole story of Lily and I."

A fear so deep ran through every single nerve cell in her body. Was he about to tell her he loved Lily and would send her away? "I'm not sure I want to know." *Not if it means I have to leave here!*

"I insist. You have a right to know why I've been going to her room every night. It isn't right or proper and if anyone starts rumors, which I'm sure they will, I want you to know the truth."

"Did something happen at the post office?"

"No. I watched Lily get thrown out of her room at the saloon this morning and realized that when I didn't go see her last night, it made the owner angry to lose the money I had been giving her. Lily is feisty and when she stood up to the new owner, the lady ousted her right out the door. A blessing in disguise if you ask me. I've been trying to help her leave there for months."

Grace remembered something about an agreement between the two when Miss Addie spoke to her before. A twinge of jealousy soured her stomach. How could that be?

"When I began to have nightmares, I would walk the streets at night to keep awake. Lily saw me and we began to talk. She has been in love with my brother Ben since the first time she saw him. Trust me on this, you'll find out he is in love with her, although too stubborn to admit he is. I promised I'd watch out for her when he left. At first, I would drink in the saloon and she'd find me after her shift and keep me from the recurring nightmares. But then the new owner wanted her to turn tricks to pay for the free room the previous owner gave her. I pretended to pay for her each night to keep her from that. We both helped each other, nothing more. The money I gave her was savings I had separate from my business."

Grace didn't indulge the fact Miss Addie had already told her some of the story. "Thank you for being honest. Now, we have work to do, are you ready?"

Dawson stared at her as if he expected shock and disbelief. Then a chuckle arose in his throat and he flung back his head and roared with laughter. He stood up, wrapped his arms around her waist and picked her up in his arms, spinning her around in circles. "You are amazing, Grace."

Her hands reached out and pulled his shirt front towards closer. She closed her eyes for the kiss about to happen. She knew a lady should wait to be kissed but not her. Grace lived in the moment and the heady feeling prompted her to want to kiss him.

A knock on the kitchen door stopped the kiss dead in its tracks. The two quickly righted themselves and swung towards the two men seen through the window. The one had his nose almost plastered against the glass pane, trying to look in. Grace giggled at his flattened nose. "We better behave. Go answer the door, husband."

"Wife." He bowed to her before heading towards the door. A bounce in his step put a big smile on her face. He was coming around. She looked up. *Thank you, Lord. You work miracles at times when things look bleak.*

<> <>

Two hours later Dawson was back with the two men who were helping to move furniture. Another crowd came in behind him as Grace stared at the front door.

She went up to her husband, placing a hand on his shoulder, speaking softly. "Who are all these people?"

An arm slaked around her waist. "Grace, meet the town of Wichita Falls. When these fine folk heard we needed some help, everyone stopped what they were doing and offered their services."

As the crowd split to let someone to the front, Grace squealed before she began to jump up and down. She slipped from Dawson's arm to hug her old friend, Ruby. While careful of the baby bump, the two began to catch up. Grace had known Ruby came to this area, but hadn't realized she was so close. "This is wonderful!"

"I can't help move anything but I'd be happy to stay here and cook us up a hearty dinner. Miss Addie and Lily are here to help. Billy, too."

The boy who delivered her parcel from the mercantile slipped from behind Ruby's skirts. "Howdy, ma'am," he said, tipping his hat like a real cowboy.

Grace scooted down and held out her hand. "Hello, young man. Thank you for delivering my package. There is some hard candy in the dish on the table in the office. Be sure to help yourself."

He nodded and moved back behind Ruby's skirt. Ruby shrugged her shoulders, her hands holding her stomach. "Well, then, let's get started. Ladies?"

Almost instantaneously, the crowd thinned out. The men worked in twos as Dawson directed them to what furniture had to be moved to the empty stage house. Grace stood in the middle of the room watching the action, surprise and awe on her face.

Ruby smiled at her, placing a basket on the table. Three other ladies began to contribute items as they stoked up the fire for cooking. Miss Addie and Lily worked together, laughing and talking as they added flour to a big bowl, stirring it with their hands. "Get used to us, Grace. We all work as a team. This town is one big family."

Grace, used to doing things on her own, let a tear fall. "Thank you." She wiped it away before slipping from the house to direct the men where to place the furniture. Shoes pounded the street, sending puffs of dust around her feet as she made her way to the staged house. Several men were dragging a settee through the front door. "Careful," she told them, scurrying up the two steps to make sure they didn't scuff the wood. Grace assessed the room and began to direct the men, sometimes having them moving things two or three times until satisfied.

At one point, Dawson leaned against the door, watching her. She twirled around, biting her bottom lip. He had never looked at her with such intensity before. Grace placed a hand to her cheek, wondering how red her face was. Blinking her eyes, she turned back to the men. *I think my husband is flirting with me!*

When she looked back, he was gone. A smile played on her lips. Maybe they would share the wedding bed tonight. Scared out of her wits and yet excited to the same degree, Grace spent the next few hours in anticipation. She was starting to feel as if she truly belonged here, as if this were her purpose.

After the men finished with the furniture, Grace put some finishing touches on the tables. She pondered for a bit, deciding to take some money from her savings to buy fresh flowers for the open house. When she heard a noise at the front door, Miss Addie and Lily were on the porch, their arms filled with flower pots. Curious, Grace went outside to see what they were doing.

"Grace, will you take a look at this?" Miss Addie stood back to show her. She had taken some of her beloved pots from her own porch to decorate this one.

She gave Miss Addie a hug. "Thank you for being so kind. I know this will help Dawson's business. I will never forget the kindness this town has shown."

Lily stepped forward. Being so close, Grace noticed her beauty. Even though her hair was pulled back in a tight bun, her sun-kissed skin and long dark eyelashes made the woman look European. Grace gave her a smile. "Thank you for everything," she told Lily in a soft voice.

"My pleasure, Grace. I hope you won't hold it against me."

"Not at all. I know about Ben. Dawson told me as much."

Lily hung her head at the mention of his name. "I have to go," she said, abruptly turning, flouncing down the steps as if someone were chasing behind.

Miss Addie placed a pointed finger over her mouth. "Touchy subject, Grace. We don't discuss Ben."

Grace flinched. "I am so sorry. Should I go talk to her?"

Miss Addie shook her head vehemently. "Leave her be, she'll be fine. Why don't you finish up and come have some dinner. We are waiting on the men to high-tail it back from the saloon. Seems like a tradition around here to buy the help a round of drinks. The men think we aren't aware of what they are doing. It won't be long, they have one glass and will be back to eat. Seems the stomach is stronger than imbibing."

After Miss Addie left, Grace checked the rooms one more time. She peeked out the window in the back of the house to find some clusters of flowers in the grass, which were perfect to cut and use on the tables inside. Using those cut flowers would save her from purchasing any. Curious, she made her way to the outside and walked down to the corner, turning back the side street to go around to the back of the house. Looking up, she noticed a face watching her from the window next door .

Sitting alone on the deserted street was a nice sized log cabin. It looked rather odd by itself and Grace remembered how Dawson told her it was one of their holdings. She stopped to stare, calculating the numbers in her head. Grace had checked and double checked all the inventory. Now that she stood staring at this strange place, the thought occurred to her there was nothing in the books that rectified for this place, even though Dawson told her it belonged to them.

Somewhere a door slammed bringing Grace back to the present. Startled, she watched a tall, thin body in men's britches stomp across the wooden porch in pointy boots with a spur hanging on the back of one. A leather belt was tied around the waist. Wearing an over large cowboy hat, it hung down so low on the person's face, it was a wonder the person didn't stumble right off the porch.

The cowboy was headed her way. The sun began to fade as it took its place behind the clouds, the sky starting to darken. Grace looked around, noticing the deserted street, wondering why the person was heading her way. Apprehension worked its way over Grace as she stepped back. Maybe she should turn and flee.

"Whoa, right there Mrs. Sloan!"

The voice didn't sound like a man but a young person. Curiosity had the best of her, so Grace looked up to see a young lady coming right at her in men's clothing. Not to say she wasn't shocked but it surprised her to no end. What was this woman doing wearing men's clothes?

"I beg your pardon?" Grace asked, trying to be civil.

"Here." She held a thick package in her hand. "You tell your husband he can't bribe the Fisher family. What's done is done!"

Grace didn't know what to do so she held out her hand. The girl slapped the package in to her palm. When Grace looked to see what was in the package, her head flew up in shock. "Where did you get this much money?"

The girl, all five foot of her, stood before Grace, her feet apart, hands on her hips. It was a comical sight since she had never seen anyone in men's clothing before. She didn't dare laugh at her, clearly the woman was troubled.

"Mr. Sloan is trying to coerce us to forgive him."

"My husband? Please tell me."

She stomped her foot then began to tap it on the ground, her pointy tip of the boot stopping now and again to dig it in the dirt. "I would think you already heard about the atrocity that happened. My sisters died at the hands of outlaws and it was his fault."

Grace gasped. "No, don't say so. It wasn't his fault. What's your name?"

She stomped her foot again. "Hannah Fisher. I was there, at the creek. I saw what happened."

"Oh my, Hannah. Please, please, you can't blame Dawson. He didn't sell the land, the Murphy boy did by mistake. Don't you see, it was all a mistake."

Hannah stared at Grace with a fire in her eye that wouldn't go out. Grace was afraid. She had never seen anyone look so horribly angry. "A mistake that cost my sisters their lives."

"Where are your parents, Hannah?" The girl couldn't be more than fourteen or fifteen.

"Not home. My dad works at the livery and my mom, I don't know. She doesn't come home until late then goes to bed. Sometimes she doesn't get out of bed at all. It's his fault. Ever since it happened, they've changed."

Grace tried to reach out to touch the sleeve of Hannah's arm but the girl slapped her hand away. Grace almost stumbled backwards.

"You tell him to keep his darn money. We don't need it or want it. Every month he leaves a pile of money on our porch. Pa says we need to give it back but Ma hides it in the cupboard and tells him she did. Do you see what he's doing to our family? It's never been spent, nary a dime. It never will be. He can't make up for what happened with bribery. You tell Mr. Sloan to go to hell."

With those harsh parting words, Hannah ran down the street, turning the corner before Grace could utter a word. Her hand flew to her forehead. Grace was trying to figure it all out. She stared at the make-shift paper bag filled with money. Dawson hadn't been making a profit because he had been giving it all away to the family he felt responsible for. Now she knew why there was no receipt for the sale of the cabin. He had never sold it. Dawson let them live there for free. As an accountant she knew he couldn't go on much longer giving away his profit. Sooner or later, it would all come crashing down. Evidently, his brother knew as well. Dawson was letting his heart rule his head.

She slumped against the side of the house, gripping on to the pile of money for dear life. If she hands this back to Dawson, his world would come crashing down. He was starting to make progress.

Grace closed her eyes, praying for a miracle to shine down from above. There had to be a way to make everything right. *Lord, show me how.*

A few seconds later she heard her name being called. Grace shot back around the corner, stuffing the money in to the deep pocket of her dress. For now, it would stay right there until she could speak to Mr. and Mrs. Fisher. Somehow, she had to make them understand this wasn't Dawsons fault. The girl was a haunted soul, filled with anger and hate towards someone she didn't know. She had to smooth things out.

"There you are. What are you doing behind the house?" Dawson asked. He stood on the wooden walkway in front of the staged property.

"I saw some flowers out back but realized it was getting dark. I want to pick them for Saturday." She hurried towards him, out of breath.

He gathered her hands in his. "Are you sure? You look out of sorts."

"I'm fine." She forced a smile, pushing the loose hair from her face. He lifted a hand to help.

"I want to kiss you, Mrs. Sloan."

"It's getting late, we should go in for dinner." Grace worried he would wrap his arms around her waist and discover the bulge in her dress where the money was hidden.

"Just one small kiss."

She reached up and gave him a small peck on the cheek, her fingers fluttering across his skin. "That is all you get for now, Mr. Sloan. Let's hurry, I'm getting hungry." She began to hurry up the street, forcing him to fall in along side of her.

"What's the hurry? You sure you are okay?"

His voice did sound concerned.

"I'm fine."

"I still want to kiss you."

"You're a good man, Dawson. I'll give you all the kisses you want after dinner and when our company leaves."

He grabbed her hand and pulled her to a stop. "Promise?" he asked, his intent gaze staring at her mouth.

"Swear to all that's right in the world, I will."

He stood still as if frozen to the spot, holding on to her. After a moment, he dropped her hand. "Well, then, Mrs. Sloan, we have some guests to be rid of."

Bypassing the office, they turned the corner and marched up the steps. Dawson pulled open the door for her. As she walked through to the delight of her guests, she swore she felt a hand sweep across her backside.

She had a feeling tonight was the night she would truly become Mrs. Dawson Sloan and nothing would stop them.

Chapter 7

Dawson was so content these past few days he was sure he would fall over from the disbelief of the way his life was turning out. He sat at his desk, staring out the window, watching the early morning sun rise. A satisfied grin rose up thinking about his wife. She was his true wife, in all areas now. No longer solely the accountant for his finances but the one he was starting to have deep feelings for. Perhaps even love.

He pushed a hand through his hair before leaning back in the chair. Was he allowing these feelings to surface without regrets for his past? It seemed as if what happened, the nightmares, the horror, were slipping away. It took Grace to make him feel something else.

She brought him back to life. The night she held him in his arms was the catapult that started it all. For six months he tortured himself, praying for an end to his misery. He did all he knew how to do to make things right. He gave the Fishers a new home, away from the murder scene. They accepted because they had no where else, Mr. Fisher told him. He didn't want Dawson's charity. Dawson didn't know what else to do when things began to spiral out of control so he dropped off money every single month.

The late night drinking and nightmares had caused him not only to tear his company to the ground but to foolishly give money away. Money he needed to keep Ben from closing the shop. Now that Grace saved him from himself, he started to realize this. Perhaps it was time to have a talk with the Fishers. Make things right. Let them know how sorry he was. He had never said it once. All he did was throw money at them, now realizing he should have done more sincerity-wise.

Sometimes he was a fool. A new determination fizzled through his bones. Dawson would make his life right again, no matter what it took. As long as Grace was by his side, he felt as if he were on top of the world. Tonight, he would tell he loved her.

Because he did.

Dawson felt the whoosh of air as the back door quietly opened and closed. His beautiful wife came sweeping through the entrance. He tilted his head and stood. She seemed shy today as he noticed the way she stood in front of him, not looking up. He had left her sleeping in their marriage bed this morning, now he wondered if he hadn't done something wrong. "Grace, did I hurt you?" he asked tenderly, reaching out to place a hand on her shoulder.

She looked up at him and smiled, placing a warm hand over top his own. "No, Mr. Sloan, you are wonderful. I'm feeling a bit shy this morning is all."

He gathered her in his arms. "Don't every feel that way around me. Tonight, I want to tell you something that's been on my mind for some time. No cooking for you, wife. We'll dine at the new place that just opened up."

"You are courting me after we have been married?" she said, teasing.

"Yes, ma'am. Dawson Sloan at your service." He stepped back and took a deep bow.

She began to head towards the door, her face shining with laughter. "I'll be back later."

"Where you going, my love?" he asked, realizing in that moment what he said to her. She stopped cold. Swung around with eyes wide open.

Her hand went to her mouth and she gasped. A giggle erupted from her throat before the widest smile crossed her face. "I'm going to make a difference," she said before closing the door behind. The jingle of the bell sounded in his head for some time before Dawson realized she was gone.

What did she mean she was going to make a difference? He shook his head. It was time to go see Mr. Fisher at the livery. Perhaps he could make things right if he apologized for all that happened.

The bell went off again. This time a stranger entered. "Hello. I'd like some information on Saturday's open house."

Dawson wished Grace would be here to talk to this guy. He sighed, picking up the brochure she had made up for the event on Saturday. He'd give the guy what he wanted and get him out of here as Dawson was anxious to make things right with the Fishers. It was time.

<> <>

Grace felt on top of the world. Her steps lightened as she walked down the boarded walk, nodding and greeting townsfolk who were starting to recognize her face. She gripped on to the reticule that held the Fisher money. She was going to go see Mr. Fisher at the livery and let him know how tortured Dawson was feeling about this whole thing. She had a hunch they were kind people. Everyone in this town was hard-working townsfolk who wouldn't deliberately hurt someone else. It was why she had to tell them about how Dawson suffered over their loss. Mayhap she was interfering but it couldn't be helped.

If Dawson found out the girl handed the money back, it would devastate him. He was a kind soul, not cruel like Hannah had made him out to be. He didn't try to bribe them with money. She didn't believe it was so even though the bulk of dollars was in her reticule. Perhaps he felt it was a small gesture to help get them back on their feet. Confusion began to eat away at Grace as she walked further down the street. She wanted to do the right thing all around.

The livery was at the very end of town, along the main street right when a traveler would enter Wichita Falls. It was a long walk but she didn't feel anxious to be going about on her own. As she entered the staples, Grace wondered again if she were doing the right thing. A few horses neighed as she walked by. She pulled up her skirts, realizing the bottom hem was dragging along the dusty ground.

The place seemed empty until she noticed a man bent over in one of the stalls. He was brushing a dark horse, lovingly placing a hand to its mane and speaking softly to the skittish mare. Grace watched for a few moments. He had an amazing talent. She noticed his eyes, they were warm and the softness at which he treated the horse was amazing.

It all changed when he looked up. Those same soft eyes stared at her with a haunting in them she couldn't describe. A hardness began to develop right before her eyes. She stepped back.

"What can I do for you?"

Grace heard a slight accent to his voice. "I would like to discuss a matter with Mr. Fisher. Are you Mr. Fisher?"

"Indeed." He continued to stroke the horse with the brush.

She cleared her throat. "Well, I, um, I am Dawson Sloan's wife."

At first, he didn't say a word. The brush stopped moving. She heard his deep sigh. "What do you want?" he asked, his tone even. Grace wasn't sure if he was angry or not interested in what she had to say.

"I want you to know that Mr. Sloan has been devastated by what happened to your daughters. Are you aware that he has had nightmares every single night since the incident?"

"So have I, Mrs. Sloan. What is your point?" He shuffled around in the stall before closing the gate. He was standing in front of her but she didn't feel any fear. The man was broken. Grace wanted to give him a hug but she didn't dare.

"Look, Mr. Fisher. Dawson's dreams haunt him. He feels responsible for what happened. The money he gave you wasn't to bribe you but as compensation for your loss. He didn't know what else to do, I'm sure of this. His own business has not seen any profit to make sure your family has all it needs."

"We do just fine without that money. I gave it back."

Grace shook her head. "No, it was never given back, that would devastate Dawson. Hannah threw it at me yesterday. I have it right here." She pulled the packet from her reticule, opening the parcel to show him the pile of money.

An angry voice shot out, "I told my wife to give this back."

"Your wife needs you, Mr. Fisher. So does your daughter. They blame Dawson for what happened. He isn't to blame. He has begun to realize it wasn't his fault. If I give this money back to him, it will undo everything." She shook the money at him, her anxiety at an all time high.

The man stood in front of her, emotionless, like a dead man walking. He took another deep breath. "I know I'm supposed to care. I feel nothing, Mrs. Sloan. My heart is dead. My girls are gone. I don't know what you want me to say or do. I have work to do."

He went to turn back to the horse when her arm shot out. She held on to his sleeve. "Your wife and daughter Hannah are alive, Mr. Fisher. They need you! There is nothing you can do about your daughters, God rest their souls. They are being taken care of in heaven. You still have people here you are responsible for and you are not doing the job you were meant to. It's time to be the head of your house again and guide them in the right direction. Hannah is lost without your direction. Your wife, she doesn't care about anything, not even Hannah. Stop this right now. Take this money and give them a good life. Please." She held the pile out to him.

He stared at her. Grace began to see a formation in his eyes. As if he realized he still had been blessed with another daughter. His chin trembled but he didn't take the money. "What have I done?" he choked, his hand flying to cover his eyes. His head hung in shame.

"Mr. Fisher, you have a second chance to make things right. Please, take this." She held out the money one more time.

"No. It doesn't belong to me. Our family will survive this loss. Dawson gave us a new home to live in, that's enough. You take that money and tell Dawson Sloan I don't blame him."

Grace smiled. "I would prefer if you tell him yourself."

"Yes, ma'am. I will. Right now, I need to go see my wife and daughter." He turned and gave her a hug, hanging on to her for a few moments.

His sniffles turned to acceptance as she hugged back. "You can do this, Mr. Fisher."

She turned to go and heard a noise at the front of the livery. A man swore and cursed but Grace tried to ignore the words. After all, she was in a man's domain here. Smiling to herself, she tucked the money back in her purse, deciding to deposit the cash in the bank before she went home to Dawson. Perhaps she would keep this whole thing quiet until Mr. Fisher spoke to him.

Sometimes Grace wanted to pat herself on the back but realized it wasn't her doing at all. God gave her a gift to smooth out rough edges and today was no different. She had a bounce in her step as she made her way through town. Smiling at everyone she passed, Grace entered the bank feeling wonderful, as if her purpose for the day was fulfilled.

Once the money was safe and sound in the company account, Grace made her way back to the land office. Tonight they were going to go to dine at the new eatery across the street. She was looking forward to spending time with Dawson. She was a real wife to him now, since their consummation last night. It was wonderful and amazing and Grace's cheeks began to burn as she thought of his tender touch while walking down the street. She grinned to herself realizing if people knew what she was thinking, they wouldn't let her walk these streets any more.

The jingle of the bell had Dawson looking up. She pranced over to him and kissed him square on the mouth. His stiff body told her something was wrong. When she glanced at his desk, she saw the problem. A drawer was opened, the contents a flask of whiskey. A small gasp from Grace made no difference.

"What are you doing?" she whispered as if others could hear.

He didn't reply. He picked up the bottle, slammed the drawer and moved towards the door.

"Dawson? What's wrong? What happened?"

He stopped. Turned his head. "Maybe you can tell me," he said, his voice cold. The jingle of the bell sounded three times louder when he slammed the door and left her alone in the office.

Grace watched from the window as Dawson worked his way towards the saloon. He tucked the bottle in his jacket before moving through the swing doors. She slumped down in the chair. *What in the world just happened?*

< > < >

Dawson leaned his foot against the bar prop while the barkeep took care of other customers. After some time, the man stood in front of him.

"What'll it be, the usual?"

He nodded. Threw some coins on the bar. A bottle and a glass appeared on the bar. Dawson snatched the bottle by its neck and made his way to a dark corner of the saloon. He didn't want to socialize with anyone right now.

He sat in the shadows. His hooded eyes stared at the bottle, this demon from the moment the accident happened. Dawson never gave it a second thought before when he first picked up the bottle to drown out his misery that night so many months ago. Night after night, he would sit here and finish one, maybe two of these. Now, he realized things were getting bad again but he didn't want to take one drink.

Then why torture himself? He skewed a hand through his hair. When he left the office this morning, his plans were to go to the livery to see Fisher. He never expected to get there in time to watch his wife hanging on to the man's sleeve, talking so serious, standing so close it threw him off balance. What was she doing with him? He stood there for a few minutes watching the two but wasn't able to hear what they were talking about. Then Fisher grabbed her and gave her a hug. He saw her arms go around him and that's when he left, almost toppling a barrel outside the livery.

He had wanted to go inside the stables and smash the man's face in. Yet, the thought of doing so disturbed him. He had caused enough heartache in that family. Was this Fishers way of getting back at him? He knew the man blamed him for his daughters death but didn't think he'd stoop that low to take his wife.

Dawson stared harder at the bottle. Was it worth loosing everything he had done in the last few days to take one drink? He thought Grace cared. She had taken him down a path he never thought was possible and now to find her in another man's arms had Dawson gripping the bottle of whiskey.

He loved her. Didn't that outweigh everything?

The bottle was a demon. If he took one sip it would send him back to the hell he had been in before Grace.

Grace.

His saving Grace had been in another man's arms.

He picked up the bottle.

Stood up.

Dawson walked to the next table and slammed it down. "It's on me," he told the three surprised cowboys. He turned and walked outside, the sunlight causing him to blink. It was time to find out why his wife had been in another man's arms.

Chapter 8

Grace marched across the street to the new eatery. The big, bold letters on the front of the building stood out. It read, *Jemma's Cafe.* She could see the newly painted words from the other side of the boarded walk.

"Welcome to Jenna's Cafe. Would you like a table for one?" the proprietor asked.

"Two. I'm meeting my husband, Mr. Dawson Sloan."

"Follow me, please." Grace followed the young lady who appeared younger than her to a quaint table tucked in to the corner of the room. A candle flickered in the middle, while two place settings were arranged on the tablecloth. "My name is Jenna, I'll be your hostess. Thank you for coming. Would you like something to drink while you wait?"

Grace smiled at the young woman. She was serious and didn't crack a smile. "No, thank you. Is this your establishment?"

The woman nodded. "It is. My brother and I had it built. He's the chef as you will see, his cooking will melt your heart." A smile finally crossed the lady's face when she spoke of her brother.

"I'll wait to order until my husband arrives. I am not sure why he is late." Except Grace knew why. He was in the saloon. She had stood at the window, waiting to see if he realized his mistake but after an hour she stopped watching. Dallying all day in her kitchen, she finally cleaned up and waited for him to return home. After he didn't show up, she decided to keep their dinner date anyway.

Grace would be the talk of the town if Dawson forgot they were dining here. But she didn't care. She was trying to go on as usual no matter what he did. If he drank today, it would start all over again. Where did that leave her? Was she supposed to stand by his side while he fell apart all over again? No. She would not do so. Determination ruled the roost. Grace would get to the bottom of things, starting with the reason he felt the need to walk back in to that saloon. It hadn't been the nightmares, they had stopped altogether. Something happened today while he was out and about. Still, it was no excuse to start drinking again.

She had thought about marching across the street to the saloon to confront him but then decided against doing so. No lady would enter a saloon, although secretly she wanted to see the inside of one. Did that make her a bad person? Grace had a knack for curiosity, sometimes it got her in trouble and she bet she wasn't the only lady in town who wondered what it looked like in there. Not even sure why she wanted to know, she stifled a grin, picking up the menu on the table.

Time was going by at a snail's pace. Grace didn't know how long she could wait. It was dark outside now, the moon shining through the front window of the restaurant. Other townsfolk were having dinner, gazing over to her table to see her sitting alone in the back, waiting on a husband she wasn't sure would show.

Jenna placed a small bowl of soup on the table. "I think this should hold you over for some time," she told Grace, patting her hand. "It's on the house."

"Thanks." Grace was hungry. She was mad, too. She had left Dawson a note to say she would meet him here as planned. But, he either hadn't seen it yet or he chose to ignore her request.

Another hour went by. Disappointed, Grace stood up to leave. He wasn't coming. She may as well face reality. "I'm leaving now," she told Jenna. "If he would happen to come by, please tell him I went home."

Jenna walked her to the door. "I will. I'm sorry, I'll smooth things over here, offer some excuse why you were alone. I know how the townsfolk talk."

She turned to leave. "Thank you."

Grace didn't feel like going home. She stood on the boarded walk staring at the darkened office. There was no light from the back, so she knew he had never made it home. She began to wander down the street, past the church and parish. Perhaps she'd check on the staged house, make sure everything was ready for Saturday night.

A feeling of doom arose inside of Grace as she placed one step in front of the other. Her shawl kept her shoulders warm but she pulled it tighter. Where was Dawson? Would he do this to her on a nightly basis? She didn't know what to do. Inside of the staged home, she struck a match and lit the lantern hanging on the wall right inside the door.

The darkness evaporated as she walked through the house with the portable oil lantern, not knowing why she was there because everything was fine, the house was staged perfectly. Whatever amount of money this sale would bring was one hundred percent profit. Grace loved the thought of making a tidy sum from one sale. The one good thing from today was after depositing the money from Mr. Fisher in the bank earlier, they were now making a profit. Dawson's brother would be happy and wouldn't try to take the business away.

Wandering to the window at the back of the house, Grace peeked out towards the Fisher cabin. She hoped and prayed they made things right and the family could begin to heal. A dim light shone through the window as several silhouettes crossed the large framed opening. Grace pressed her nose to the cold glass, trying to make out a face. She wanted to see what Mrs. Fisher looked like but the shadows weren't clear enough. She promised herself to call upon them in the near future.

Grace placed the lamp back, bending slightly as she blew out the flame, working her way outside to the porch. She looked around, realizing too late how dark it seemed. Modern street lamps like in New York City would be so helpful here. Perhaps she should suggest it at a town meeting, if they had any.

Beside her, soft music flowed from Miss Addie's boarding house. She heard a variety of voices singing along, the sound flowing through the open window. Grace sat on the front porch step listening, humming along, not wanting to disturb Miss Addie and her guests. She'd sit for awhile and let the music sooth her soul before returning to an empty house.

Grace heard the footsteps before seeing who they belonged to. They were slow and steady, so she turned towards the corner of the house as someone's boots hit the dirt coming from the direction of the cabin. Should she be alarmed? Grace had never been out alone at night. She tucked herself in to the corner of the step, hoping whoever passed by wouldn't notice her since there was no time to go inside.

The boots hesitated before stopping in front of the porch. Grace was nervous and curious at the same time, thinking it may be one of the Fishers. She peeked her head out from the steps to find her husband standing there, staring at the house. She didn't think he noticed her sitting alone in the dark. The soft music stopped for a brief moment to be replaced by some bouncy piano tune. The voices inside became louder. Grace tried to stay still but her foot began to tap against the wooden step.

"I see you, Grace. What are you doing out alone?"

She stood. "I didn't want to go home to an empty house."

"I am ashamed, Grace. I haven't been home, trying to figure things out. I went to see the Fishers."

"We had a date."

She heard the intake of his breath, the surprise in his voice. "I'm so sorry, Grace. I forgot."

Grace went to him. "Will you always forget me whenever you have something going on?"

He swung towards her. "Never, Grace. When I left today, I was so mad that I had to get away. I didn't want you to see me so angry and hurt at what I thought you did."

"Why were you mad? What did you think I did?" Confused, Grace pulled on her shawl, instantly tightening it around her. She hadn't done a thing to him.

Hesitating at first, he turned towards the street. "Grace, I am ashamed to admit I thought you betrayed me."

"What! I'd never do so! Dawson, how could you!"

"I know, I was wrong. When I went to the livery this morning, I saw you in Fisher's arms. It crushed me, Grace. I thought you cared and when I saw him holding you, it killed me."

Anger flashed in her eyes. "I gave the man a hug. He's been through so much and he agreed to talk to you about what happened. If you came upon us, you should have stayed to find out the real reason I was there."

"I know, Grace. I am weak about anything to do with the Fishers. Afterwards, I went to the saloon and sat there for hours, contemplating a drink. In the end, it wasn't worth taking a swallow. I left there and walked and walked, winding up at the Fishers. I just left there. I'm so sorry I missed our dinner together. Forgive me, Grace."

She stared at him, knowing he was truly sorry and yet anguished at what to do. He couldn't be allowed to treat her so lightly, no matter what he was going through. "I do forgive you, Dawson and I'm glad you made things right with the Fishers. With me, however, it may take some time to get over things. I'm not happy at all at being stood up by my husband. I'll be the talk of the town come morning." With that, she mustered up all the energy she could, turned and marched down the street, holding her skirts out of the dirt.

He followed behind, catching up within a few seconds. "Grace, what can I do to make this up to you?" He caught her elbow and swung her around. She all but fell in to his arms. Looking up at his handsome face, she almost gave in. What she wanted to do was plant a kiss on him but she didn't. He couldn't get away with treating her so badly. Even though a wife must accept any of her husband's discretions, she always thought that was nonsense and she was having non of it, no way. She was a modern woman and wouldn't put up with any shenanigans.

She pulled away. "Dawson Sloan, it may take lots of flowers and sweet talk to convince me you are truly sorry. The chocolate at the mercantile, you know, those imported from Belgium would help also. Goodnight, it's going to be a long day tomorrow."

Grace hurried inside so he didn't follow. She wanted him to suffer some to learn his lesson but wound up being the one to suffer alone in bed. She opened her eyes during the night to find him by the fire, rocking back and forth. When she stirred in bed, moving over to make room, she called out for him to come to bed, he turned to her and grinned, a content look on his face.

"Go back to sleep, Grace. We have a busy day tomorrow."

"I forgive you, Dawson. Come to bed."

"No Grace, shh, go to sleep."

Grace tossed and turned for some time, realizing he turned the tables on her. A slight smile covered her face as she drifted off.

<> <>

Something tickled her nose. She looked down on the blanket to find a set of brown eyes staring at her. They were round and scared and attached to a brown puppy so cute she cried out. Sitting up in bed, Grace gathered the little thing in her arms. It was so tiny and soft. She looked around for her husband but he was gone. Disappeared.

He brought her a puppy.

Score one point for the husband.

Grace played with the puppy, giggling as it became curious and chased her hand all over the quilt. When she heard the noise at the door, she looked up to find Dawson holding a tray in his hands.

"How did I do?"

She laughed out loud. "Beautiful, so far. A puppy is much better than flowers or chocolates, although I love them, too."

He entered the room, setting the tray on her lap. A single flower in a makeshift cup graced the meal. "How about breakfast? Would that give me points?"

"Maybe." The curious puppy sniffed at the plate, his tongue slaking out to capture the eggs on the plate. Grace pulled a little piece off, feeding the puppy the soft food.

"Thank you."

"I love you, Grace. I don't want to lose you and I'll do anything to make things better."

She turned to him. "You love me, Dawson? Truly?"

"Yes. I am in love with my beautiful wife." He knelt down at the side of the bed, taking her hand in his.

The puppy ignored, she placed a hand over his cheek. "I love you too, Dawson. Please, don't ever go in to the saloon like you did. Promise me you will talk to me first before getting upset."

He sat on the bed, by her side, taking her in his arms. "I promise, my love, I will never do something as foolish as to think you want another man. When I talked to Fisher and he explained everything, I realized right away what a fool I was. I can't promise you a perfect marriage, but I'll do my best to make you happy, to care for you as you deserve and to provide you with a home like no one else can. You have my word."

Grace knew it was the beginning of a whole new life. Her husband had finally come around, forgiving his past and able to move forward. "I promise, Mr. Sloan, to stick by your side, no matter the cost, whatever it is or what challenges lie ahead, I am always here, your wife and true love."

She kissed him then, full on his mouth and with every ounce of love inside her heart. When the wet tongue slid across her cheek she jumped back in shock. The puppy jumped on her while he continued to lick her and yelp.

Dawson and Grace rolled across the bed, laughter rising from deep in their souls. The puppy ran over them both, bouncing and yelping, drawing the laughter from deeper inside. It was a great day to be alive.

<> <>

"Ben." Dawson watched him walk in to the staged house. Bigger than life, he had an air about him like no other in this small town of Wichita Falls. The man was well dressed, a gentleman and his big brother. People stopped to stare at the man who came through the door. Dawson excused himself.

"Dawson," his brother said, his deep voice reverberating through the room. The brothers shook hands and then hugged, patting each other on the back.

"It's great to see you, Ben."

"Likewise. I see you have the business back to normal." He turned to look around the room, nodding at several townsfolk.

"Come meet my wife." Ben followed him to the small crowd surrounding his beautiful wife. "This is Ben Sloan, Grace. My brother."

Grace, graceful as always, held out her hand. He watched in amusement as Ben took her hand, kissed it and then pulled her to him for a hug. "Welcome to the family, sister. I hear you tamed my little brother."

She laughed out loud. "It didn't take a whole lot," she swore, staring at Ben. "You have a fine brother. I'm proud to be his wife."

Ben nodded. "Thank you." As if there were an unspoken language between the two, Grace turned and smiled at him. *I love you*, she mouth before returning to the others.

He stood beside his brother, watching the crowd. "This whole thing is Grace's idea, Ben. She staged the furniture and invited everyone within twenty miles of Wichita Falls to come see the house for sale."

"Brilliant idea. I can see she compliments you." Ben turned to him. "I'm sorry for what you had to deal with, Dawson. I wasn't trying to shut you down, honest. I just needed you to grow up and stop blaming yourself for the murders. It was never your fault."

"I see that now. Grace helped me. I've got a good life here, Ben. Why don't you stay. Forget Fort Worth. Make this your home."

A distant look came in to his brother's eyes. Dawson knew he was thinking of Lily. The two had loved each other for a long time but something had happened. Neither one would tell him.

Dawson knew the moment Lily stepped in to the room when Ben's eyes glazed over. The need and want he saw there was the same Dawson felt for his wife.

Then Ben announced his plans, so loud and clear Lily heard him loud and clear all the way from the other side of the room. "I am back, Dawson. I bought the hotel next to Jenna's Cafe."

"That's great, brother!" Dawson slapped him on the back, amused at the unspoken exchange he was witnessing between his brother and Lily.

Ben was no longer looking at Dawson. He kept his eyes on Lily as he made the next announcement. She stared back so hard, her dark eyes were wide open, the longing there for all to see. "I'm going to do the same thing you did, Dawson. I'm going to order me a mail order bride."

The crowd in the room got quiet. Everyone looked at Lily. Dawson thought it was petty and mean of Ben to make such an announcement in front of Lily. After all, the two had been in love with each other for a long time before he had gone away so suddenly.

"That's not right, brother."

"Maybe not, but perhaps the woman will come to her senses. I've asked her for the last three years to marry me. I've sent her letters to have them sent back unopened. If she doesn't do something soon, I will marry a mail order bride. I'm tired of being alone. I want a wife like you have."

Dawson turned to his wife. She was the best thing that ever happened to him. *I love you*, he mouthed to her before heading outside to show his brother more of their holdings. He had a great life now, with a beautiful wife and living in a town he was proud of.

It was a great life. A great day to be alive.

<><> Thank you for reading Grace <><>

Keep reading - Ben and Lily's story is next!

What's Next in Wichita Falls?

Next up is Ben Sloan and Lily Morgan. Can they work out their
differences before it's too late? Will Ben take up a mail order bride
and lose the woman he has always loved?
Find out in Lily: Mail Order Brides of Wichita Falls
Now Available exclusively at Amazon[1] (http://amzn.to/
1UKgJph)
Click here to download[2] (http://amzn.to/1UKgJph)
or get Volume 1
Mail Order Brides Box set Volume 1[3] (https://www.amazon.com/
gp/product/B076YXYBN8)

Have you read the exclusive reader story about Miss Addie at
www.cyndiraye.com and how she came to Wichita Falls yet?
If not, get her story here FREE for my reader's only!
Get Miss [4]Addie[5]'s Story here[6] (http://www.cyndiraye.com/
miss-addies-story/)

---

1. http://amzn.to/1UKgJph

2. http://amzn.to/1UKgJph

3. https://www.amazon.com/gp/product/B076YXYBN8

4. http://www.cyndiraye.com/miss-addies-story/

5. http://www.cyndiraye.com/miss-addies-story/

6. http://www.cyndiraye.com/miss-addies-story/

I'd love it if you joined our reader's group on [7]Facebook[8] Click here to join![9] (https://www.facebook.com/groups/1856224058000936/)

*****

Books by Cyndi Raye
Mail Order Brides of Wichita Falls Series
Ruby
Grace
Lily
Charity
Hannah
Rebecca
Sophie
Ellie
Jenna
Leila
Boxed Set Vol 1-8
Christmas in Wichita Falls Holiday Book
Brides of Mill Ridge Series
An Outlaws Honor
A Reverend's Rose
The Ranger's Redemption
A Doctor's Devotion
A Teacher's Treasure
A Sister's Sanctuary

---

7. https://www.facebook.com/groups/1856224058000936/

8. https://www.facebook.com/groups/1856224058000936/

9. https://www.facebook.com/groups/1856224058000936/

Sons of Nora White Series
A Bride for Luke
A Bride for Adam
A Bride for Samuel
A Groom for Nora
A Bride for Russell
A Bride for Wesley
A Groom for Widow Young
Multi-Author Series Contributions
A Bride for Abel - The Proxy Brides
A Bride for Calvin - The Proxy Brides
A Tin Star for Christmas - The Belles of Wyoming
Candy Cane Christmas - Ornamental Matchmaker Book #10
An Agent for Cari - The Pinkerton Matchmakers
An Agent for Carolina - The Pinkerton Matchmakers
Pistol Ridge Series
Peg Leg's Princess
Blaze's Beauty
Judge's Jewel
Rider's Renegade
Creed's Confidant
Raven's Rebel
Preacher's Pearl

All these books can be found by visiting
https://www.amazon.com/Cyndi-Raye/e/B00ENA1WEG

Don't miss out!

Visit the website below and you can sign up to receive emails whenever Cyndi Raye publishes a new book. There's no charge and no obligation.

https://books2read.com/r/B-A-PXQ-EFMFC

BOOKS 2 READ

Connecting independent readers to independent writers.

9 798215 684092